What the critics are saying:

"I honestly loved this book." - *Dani Jacquel, Just Erotic Romance Reviews*

"The sex is hotter than hot and will keep you squirming in your seat. Price of Fame is another great book to add to Ashley Ladd's growing list." - *Angel Brewer, Just Erotic Romance Reviews*

"Ms. Ladd delivers a remarkable story of the perils of being a rock and roll star by night and an average female by day. It has all of the makings of a hit; humor, suspense, romance, passion, and some good old fashioned romper room sex. Ms. Ladd has just earned a new spot on my favorites list." - *Ansley, Sizzling Romance Review*

"Ashley Ladd showcases her writing talents in this classic Cinderella fable. In my opinion, the writing is first class. The only thing I didn't like about the story was the mother and sister...but where would Cinderella have been without her wicked stepmother and stepsisters? If you want a contemporary look as a classic fable...don't miss The Price of Fame." - *Jennifer Ray, The Road to Romance*

Price of Fame

Ashley Ladd

PRICE OF FAME
An Ellora's Cave Publication, December 2004

Ellora's Cave Publishing, Inc.
1337 Commerce Drive, Suite #13
Stow, Ohio 44224

ISBN #1419950959
Other available formats: MS Reader (LIT), Adobe (PDF),
Rocketbook (RB), Mobipocket (PRC) & HTML

Edited by *Briana St. James*
Cover art by *Darrell King*

Warning:

The following material contains graphic sexual content meant for mature readers. *Price of Fame* has been rated *E–rotic* by a minimum of three independent reviewers.

Ellora's Cave Publishing offers three levels of Romantica™ reading entertainment: S (S-ensuous), E (E-rotic), and X (X-treme).

S-*ensuous* love scenes are explicit and leave nothing to the imagination.

E-*rotic* love scenes are explicit, leave nothing to the imagination, and are high in volume per the overall word count. In addition, some E-rated titles might contain fantasy material that some readers find objectionable, such as bondage, submission, same sex encounters, forced seductions, etc. E-rated titles are the most graphic titles we carry; it is common, for instance, for an author to use words such as "fucking", "cock", "pussy", etc., within their work of literature.

X-*treme* titles differ from E-rated titles only in plot premise and storyline execution. Unlike E-rated titles, stories designated with the letter X tend to contain controversial subject matter not for the faint of heart.

Also by Ashley Ladd:

American Beauty
Carbon Copy

Price of Fame

Chapter One

"Skye Blue! Skye Blue! Skye Blue!" The audience chanted, demanding Skye's return to the stage. The coliseum shook with thunderous clapping and pounding feet.

"They can't get enough of you, Skye. They love you." Thunder Cloud hoisted her in his huge arms and spun her around. "Go get 'em, Tiger!"

Exhilaration swept over Wenefred "Wendy" Applegate, known to her fans only as Skye Blue. She lived to perform, to give joy to her fans, to feel the love and respect with which they flooded her. It didn't quite make up for the lack of love and respect she'd been denied by her own family, but it helped.

She hugged her friend, and squeezed his hand. Keeping tight hold on it, she pulled him with her. "Encore time!"

Lightning, Hail, and Rain, the other members of the band, followed. Hand-in-hand, they ran back onstage together, bowed, and took their places for a final song. Wendy settled behind her electric piano while Lightning and Thunder picked up their guitars. Hail took up her saxophone and strapped it over her back.

"Sing 'Depraved Love', Skye," a man in the front row screamed. Within seconds, the crowd echoed his request. The chant rang through Wendy's head and she had to take a deep breath to block it out and concentrate. 'Depraved Love' was Storm's platinum single, burning up the charts.

Thunder winked at her and placed his pluck on his electric strings, the signal to the band that he was ready to lead them into the performance. They knew this hit so well, they could play it in their sleep.

Wendy opened her mouth wide and let her voice flow. Its lush timbre and range never failed to lift her to the stars...or astound her that it could come out of such a plain, nondescript face.

She thanked God for their disguises that leant mystique and beauty to her drab features. She doubted anyone would listen to her voice if they knew it came packaged in a plain brown wrapper.

She poured all her pain and longing into the song. Pathos was her specialty. Her mother had always called her the drama queen, while her perfect sister, Angelina, was the beauty queen and the family's hope and sunshine. They looked to Angelina to bring fame, fortune, and glory to the family, not her, Wendy. Thus, she guarded her secret fanatically, especially from them. They thought she worked as a traveling salesperson for feminine hygiene products. Embarrassed, they told people she was a receptionist in the big city who shamelessly ignored her family and shunned her sister's many beauty pageants because she was jealous.

Wendy hit a particularly difficult high note and held it, caressing it. After the haunting strains of the melody faded, silence deafened the house for a long moment. She held her breath as always, awaiting the audience's reaction.

Then the crowd went wild, stomping, whistling, and screaming her name. Few artists rivaled her talent, and she knew it was her voice that had led the band to such meteoric popularity.

Thunder, Lightning, Hail, and Rain joined hands. Thunder held out his free hand to her and clasped her fingers warmly. Together, they bowed again.

Then the musician picked her up and tossed her in the air to Lightning as their light display arced around them, illuminating the coliseum. Fans flicked their lighters and a billion flames of fire flickered in the night, a mighty testament to a job well done.

Wendy's heart lurched and she squealed with laughter. "Put me down!" *Ugh, what cavemen!* But the guys ignored her, hyped up by the dynamite performance.

"What are your wives gonna say?" That little reminder sobered them and they set her on her feet. Not before Lightning's thumbs grazed her breasts, though, taking liberties he knew were off-limits.

Scowling, Thunder said, "The crowd loves it. They think we have a hot fling going."

Rain tilted her head and said dreamily, "Better yet, a love triangle."

Lightning grinned wolfishly. "Maybe even a threesome."

Shocked, Skye gaped at the guitarist. "Your wife would kill you for that." *If I don't first.*

His grin widened and his eyes twinkled. "How'd you know she wouldn't want to be part of the sandwich, luv?"

Skye gasped and she wondered if he was for real or an incorrigible tease. "You're a wicked, wicked man." She crossed her fingers in the sign of the cross. "Back, demon, before I vanquish you."

Thunder whispered in her other ear, "You know I'd love being the middle of you and Carly. Or to have you in the middle of me and Lightning."

Unsure whether to be flattered or insulted, she pretended she couldn't hear his lewd suggestion over the cacophony. He'd had his chance once and threw her over for his model-perfect, blond bimbo wife. Wendy wasn't about to be the other woman to the other woman or engage in a ménage a trois with them. Even if she was tempted, it would never be with a stunning, stacked beauty that made her look like dog meat.

But Thunder wasn't one to give up his bone easily. *Or was that his boner?* "How about tonight? We'll celebrate our awesome success, suck my dick, and then I'll take turns fucking yours and Carly's brains out."

Irked now, she flicked her wrist disdainfully. "Dream on. You had your chance." Besides, she liked her brains just where they were, thank you very much.

Her partner frowned and hung his shaggy head as they departed the stage. "And I blew it. I made a terrible mistake. She can't even string a coherent sentence together."

Skye arched her brow. "And that's somehow my fault?" Disbelieving, she wondered how she had remained good friends with such a moron. Probably because this was the first time he'd made such a lascivious advance on her. *What did he smoke before the set?*

She disappeared into her dressing room, washed her face and became just plain Wendy again, mourning the loss of her alter ego. Yet, she was thankful for her ordinary visage as it allowed her to move around incognito and lead a fairly normal life. No one but her band and manager knew her true identity.

Careful not to let anyone see her exit, she slipped out the back door. She breathed a sigh of relief that Thunder and Lightning weren't waiting to ambush her. The thought of a ménage a trois with the duo of sinfully sexy rock stars made her quiver, yet she knew it would be disastrous to sleep with her co-workers. Nor would her morals permit her to dally with married men. And contrary to Thunder's assertions to the opposite, his wife, Carly, would have both their heads if they seriously considered it.

Wendy caught a taxi back to her hotel, rejecting the limousine that most stars preferred. She wasn't a diva, although her attitude prompted many a heated argument with her manager and publicist, who wanted her to become a much more public person.

At least the paparazzi never hounded her, and she'd never had crazed fans crawling through her bedroom window. And in a perverse way, Skye Blue and Storm's secret identities propelled their popularity.

Half an hour later, she dragged herself into the hotel lobby. Dead tired, her feet swelling, she stopped by the concierge desk. "Any messages for me?"

An oak tree of a man, tall, lanky, and impeccable in a midnight blue hotel uniform, looked down his patrician nose at her as if she was a bug. "And you are?"

Oh, yeah. She was Miss Nobody again — an invisible, worthless, unmemorable, unimportant face. She should be accustomed to it by now, but it never failed to rankle. "Wenefred Applegate. Room 1214."

He reached into the cubby assigned to 1214 and pulled out an official looking document. He held it out to her as if it were a distasteful item. "Telegram for you, Mademoiselle."

She snatched it from him, her blood humming, her pulse flipping out. No one ever sent a telegram to Wendy Applegate.

"Will that be all, Mam'selle?" The man started to leave without awaiting her reply.

She ripped open the message and stood transfixed, unable to exhale. Her mother had been the victim of a serious car crash and was fighting for her life in ICU.

Her diva persona inadvertently emerged. "Garcon! Call for a car to take me to the airport. And have my bags packed immediately and sent to me at this address." She scribbled her mother's address on a scrap of paper and thrust it at him.

The man looked over his shoulder, blinking. "Excuse me?"

"You heard me. Do it." When he still hesitated, she sighed loudly and greased his palm with a crisp one-hundred-dollar bill. She dangled a second Alexander Hamilton under his nose. "If you can get my things to me in ten minutes, this is yours also."

She could see the creep's salivary glands working overtime. Greed lit his beady little eyes and his fingers twitched. Miraculously, he turned into a gracious servant, eager to do her bidding. *Funny how money worked almost as well as beauty to get one's way.*

"I'd be delighted, Mam'selle. I'll see to it myself." He snapped his fingers high in the air and crooked his head to the side to one of his lackeys.

"Very good. I'll be waiting out front." She dragged out her cell phone and hit speed dial as she strode swiftly outside. Her foot tapped rapidly as she waited for her sister to answer. "One. Two. Three. Four... Come on, Angel. Pick up!"

A bellhop crashed into her, pushing her down, and knocking the phone out of her hand. She landed on her hands and knees, her flesh stinging, her hose ripped. Pebbles imbedded in the meaty flesh of her palm, and she winced.

The young man bent down and gave her a hand up. "I'm so sorry. I didn't see you."

She tried to smile but ended up baring her fangs. "Yeah. Yeah. I'm invisible. I know." She knew she was being unforgivably rude, but her mother might be dying, and her phone lay in the cruddy gutter.

"You're short. And you're wearing dark clothes that blend into the building."

Oh, God. Now, she was a wicked old crone! "Oh."

He found her phone and handed it to her. He approached her carefully, as if fearing she was rabid.

She couldn't blame him. She had been pretty hostile. Chagrined, she offered him a smile and a thank you. Then, feeling generous, she gave him a backstage pass for the next time Storm came to town. "You like to attend rock concerts?"

The kid's eyes lit up. "Wow! Where'd you get these?"

A smile crooked her mouth. "I'm friends with their manager's secretary." The lie slid off her lips too easily. She was not the same girl who had left sleepy Palm Springs a decade before. And poor Palm Springs was about to find out.

* * * * *

Dr. Trace Cooper took Bessie Applegate's vitals. He jerked his hand back when she batted it away. The old bat was the worst patient he'd ever had. She'd tried to bite him earlier that day. But he should be used to her. She'd only lived next-door his entire life.

"I don't need damn doctors! I need my children gathered around my death bed." Bessie glared at him with her glowing feral eyes.

Angelina, her younger daughter, clutched Bessie's other hand in hers, stroking it, her exquisite face pinched. "Don't die on me, Mama. I don't know what I'd do without you."

"Has Wendy arrived yet? I swear, I don't know why my oldest child insists on peddling deodorant instead of coming to her mother's death bed." Bessie's eyes crossed as she looked down her nose at him. She shivered and drew her blanket under her chin.

Angelina pouted and helped her mother adjust her blankets more comfortably. "She's just being selfish, living on the other side of the country, traveling all the time. She's been too busy to attend any of my beauty pageants since she left home. All she cares about is her shampoo and tampons. Like, what's so important about that?"

"It's how I make my living." Soft chastisement laced the familiar voice that came from the doorway. He hadn't heard it in several years but he'd known it his entire life.

Trace's gaze jerked up and narrowed on the woman strolling to the bed with purpose. The striking vision couldn't be homely Freddie, could it? Yet, he remembered that lovely, if cynical, voice, like melted milk chocolate with a bite.

Awestruck, he tensed. The pudgy, gap-toothed, straggly-haired shrimp had been replaced by a polished, sleek, commanding woman. Perfect, shiny teeth filled her mouth, letting the sunlight come out and play in her smile. A smooth, alabaster complexion replaced the previously pimply eyesore. Sleek, raven hair glided down to the middle of her back. But the most alluring change was her body. Slim, trim, and curvy in all the right places, she was a sight to behold. She wasn't technically as beautiful as her younger sister, but she commanded definite interest.

"So, the prodigal daughter returns." Angelina's cattiness destroyed her beauty. Her lips thinned. Her flesh tightened across already taut cheeks causing her to look almost emaciated.

"It's about time, Missy. I don't know how much longer I can hold on." Bessie scooted up in the bed, propping herself up with her pillows.

Trace rushed to adjust the bed, making her as comfortable as possible. She might be a crotchety old woman, but she was still his patient and his neighbor.

"I came as soon as I got the message." Freddie leaned over and kissed her mother's withered cheek.

"I sent it two days ago. Where were you that you didn't get it?" Angelina pinned her sister with a lethal glare from the opposite side of the bed.

Watching the newcomer through his peripheral vision, he was fascinated by the new, improved version. Pretending to take Bessie's pulse gave him a reason to stay long enough to hear the answer. He also noted that the sisters' rivalry had only increased with time. An only child, he'd always envied them siblings while he was growing up, but now he wasn't so sure.

Freddie blanched, and then regained her composure swiftly. "I was out of town at a conference. My secretary was off duty for the weekend and didn't see this to forward it to me right away."

"When did you get a secretary? My, my, are we coming up in the world? Get a promotion you didn't tell us about?" Angelina's harsh tones belied her beauty and Trace didn't like what he was seeing. If this was the treatment Freddie received at home, no wonder she rarely visited.

"What is this? The inquisition? My group—my sales group, that is—shares a secretary." Freddie thrust out her impressive chest, lifted her chin regally, and parried her hostile sibling's scathing retorts adroitly.

Trace took back his initial impression that her most alluring new trait was her hard body. Although her new curves were most provocative, it was her new self-confidence that was most attractive. Yet, his pulse raced at the sight of her hardened nipples pushing against the silky fabric of her blouse.

He snapped back to reality. *Since when did he fantasize about Freddie? He was losing it. He'd been awake far too many hours.*

"Down, girls! Can't you see I'm in no shape to put up with your bickering? Show a dying woman some respect." Forceful vitality echoed in Bessie's voice, and Trace had to bite back a grin. The old dowager wasn't going to meet her maker today. The heart monitor ticked away, strong and steady, seconding his opinion.

But she was recovering from severe injuries and needed her rest. "Ladies? Your mother needs some quiet now." He patted Bessie's blue-veined hand that was fisted and ready for battle. "Try to get some sleep now, Bess."

The surly patient pierced each of her daughters with her blistering gaze. "Give your momma a kiss, girls. It may be your last chance on this Earth."

Angelina rushed to be first, and he wondered where all her grace and poise had evaporated. To Freddie, obviously, who strolled to her mother's side and hugged her warmly. "Sleep tight, Mom. I'll be here when you awaken."

"Promise? You won't go traipsing off again to save the world with a new, improved tampon?"

"Promise, Ma." Trace could hear Freddie gritting her teeth and moaned inwardly. He didn't want to get in the middle of their battle.

* * * * *

Wendy straightened as tall as she could, feeling the sting of her mother's verbal slap. Her bruised heart still ached from the force of her sister's forked tongue. She cut her some slack under the extenuating circumstances, recalling her own slip into rudeness just a few hours before. Annoyed, she didn't appreciate the barrage of antagonistic accusations. Now, was a time for family solidarity, not genocide.

Why had no one told her that he'd become a body builder? Surely, Angel would have gloated about her boyfriend being so buff. Obviously she'd been away from home too long. One didn't build a body that gorgeous overnight. Then, again, she had avoided him religiously whenever she'd visited. No sense making a fool of herself again over her teenage crush who had made it obvious that he preferred her much more beautiful younger sister.

She squeezed her mother's hand and cracked a lopsided smile. "I'll be here. Don't worry."

Trace held the door wide for her and motioned for her to precede him. His scent, so like an evergreen forest, wrapped around her, a welcome diversion from the strong hospital antiseptic that wrinkled her nose. Nor, could she help but notice the breath-taking span of his shoulders and narrow hips. His gray-blue eyes were inscrutable slabs of granite. She wondered how short she fell in his estimation of an attractive woman.

She waited up for him, even though she'd rather stay the course of avoiding him. She needed questions answered, so she fell into pace beside him as she made her way to the elevators at the end of the hall. Worry and guilt swelled in her heart. What would she do if her mother died? Their father had passed away several years before, and it had just been the Applegate women against the world ever since. "Truthfully, will she live?"

The doctor stopped and faced her. He looked down from his enormous height of 6' or so. At least it seemed enormous to her 5'1" perspective. She didn't like being so short and didn't appreciate how Thunder and Lightning thought her diminutive size so cute, they just had to toss her around like a rag doll whenever they got hyped. She wasn't cute. She was a grown woman. A successful artist. Cute wasn't in her vocabulary.

"She'll live. But she has a long road to recovery and will need complete bed rest for at least a couple months."

Months? Alarm jolted through her. She couldn't stay for months. Storm was in the midst of a huge concert tour. She had obligations. Contracts. "Are you saying that I need to be here throughout her entire recovery?"

His eyes narrowed on her and he stiffened. "Yes. That would be advisable. She needs all the love and support she can get from her loved ones."

Her mind worked furiously, trying to figure out how to handle this. "What if we hire a live-in nurse or two? And a housekeeper who can cook?"

Trace's brows quirked. "You have the money for all that?"

She gulped, and nodded slowly. She wasn't fond of flaunting her wealth, but in this case, it was necessary. "Money's not a problem."

"But I take it spending time with your own mother is?" He faced off against her and laid his hand on her forearm. "Where's the Freddie I knew?"

The electric spark his touch generated through her ignited the worry and frustration engulfing her, and she exploded at him. Shaking his hand off her arm, she blew up. She detested that awful, horrible, butt-ugly nickname. But what she hated much more was how he questioned her loyalties and sensibilities. "My name is Wendy, not Freddie. Wen-dee. Wendy. W-e-n-d-y. And how dare you insinuate that I care more for my career than for my mother." With that, she pivoted on her heel, tossed her head, and departed.

* * * * *

"Bitch!" Trace mumbled under his breath, disenchanted with the she-dragon. He needed a fireproof suit to survive her back draft. If this was her attitude, she might as well have remained across country.

"I heard that!" Freddie—no, Wendy—called after him. She walked backwards, glaring at him. "What kind of bedside manner is that for a doctor?"

He bit back the growl rising in his chest. Never had a woman infuriated him so much. He never lost his cool on the job. He could feel the blistering gazes of his coworkers on him, so he couldn't say what burned his lips. Instead, he said, "I said, I would have to switch medications."

"Uh huh. Right." Her sarcasm annoyed him no end. He'd have to do everything in his power to get Bessie well fast, so the witch could go home.

Wendy sashayed away, the sway of her hips mesmerizing him. Monopolizing the light as it bounced around her slim waist, her glossy hair beckoned his fingers to run through it.

He swore inwardly and turned away in disgust. That glorious hair and sexy hips belonged to a viper.

When his shift ended, he stopped at the gym to work off his frustrations. He pressed weights, chagrined that all he could think about was pumping something else entirely different.

Chapter Two

"Roger. I'm really stuck here." Wendy held the cell phone away from her ear when her manager resumed screeching at her that they'd be in violation of contract and committing career suicide if Storm had to cancel or reschedule their engagements.

When the fire and brimstone stopped hailing on her head, she said, "I have no choice. My mother needs me." They had moved her home from the hospital and only had two nurses on staff, not the hospital-full that Bessie had kept at her beck and call.

"So fly in once a week to visit the old darling. You can afford it. Or better yet, bring her with you." He slurped something. A chronic multi-tasker, he had a bad habit of eating while talking.

She bit back a sigh and rubbed her aching forehead. "She's too ill to move. She needs complete bed rest, peace, and quiet." Even if she were 100%, Bessie Applegate could not take the vagabond life of a roadie. And Angel's fit would make an A-bomb explosion seem mild.

"So, hire a nurse. Buy a whole friggin' hospital. Lord knows you can afford it. Do what it takes to get your sweet ass back here, pronto. We have a gig in Orlando this weekend. Surely, dear old Mummy will understand."

Maybe, if dear old Mummy knew the truth. Did she dare tell her? Now? She should come clean to her mother and explain the truth, yes. But, baring her soul, easing her conscience and uncomplicating her life would be beyond selfish under the circumstances. Once her mother was out of danger, she would tell her. Not a second before.

However, Orlando was near enough she could sneak away for an evening. Angel would just have to deal. "Okay, Rog. Stop tripping out on me. I'll be in Orlando this weekend."

"Finally, duckie. You've come to your senses." He smacked his lips loudly.

She paced, clutching the phone, cursing the technology that allowed for constant contact with her manager. "I said I could make Orlando. But, I can't go just anywhere right now." She braced herself for the fallout, holding the phone an inch away from her already throbbing ear.

"Then we're in breach. Your fans will turn on you. You can tell your band members how you're flushing their careers down the loo."

She plopped onto an overstuffed lounger and flung her legs over the arm. "You've got a mother. Surely, you can sympathize." Although, on second thought, he was probably hatched.

"Is she really that ill?"

"She's on her death bed." *She says.* Not that Wendy believed her mother was truly dying, but she was undergoing crucial recovery. "My being with her—or not—could make the difference. And my sister needs help."

"Death bed, you say? Will her doctors certify that?" He paused so long, Wendy thought he'd dropped the phone. She was ready to hang up and dial him back when he spoke again. "Maybe this could work for us. The press would eat it up. Skye Blue rushes home for Mum's dying wish."

Furious, she shot up from the lounger. The man was a complete insensitive lout. She'd have to talk to the other members of Storm about replacing him with someone who possessed a heart. "No! You're not turning my mother's illness into a three-ring circus. Plus, that would blow our secret identities."

"So, I forgot in my enthusiasm that under no circumstances can anyone see your face minus the paint. Heaven forbid anyone should see your real face."

His swearing scalded her ears, and she rolled her eyes heavenward. She hung her head and massaged her hammering temples. Maybe this was a sign that she should just retire. She had enough money to live comfortably for the rest of her life. She'd invested well. Rumor had it that Thunder was having financial difficulties and was in no position to quit yet. Of course, he would probably be snapped up by another band, but she couldn't believe a one or two-month hiatus would kill their career. They wouldn't be the first rock group to have a family emergency interrupt their tour. "Just get me out of my commitments for at least the next month. It may take even longer than that."

"What if I can move the concerts closer to you till your Mum's better? You'll have to practice, so we'll move the band down there, too."

Staring out the window, she considered the suggestion. She plucked at her mother's potted palm, shredding a frond. "Well...that might work. But I have to be here the better part of each day."

"Maybe they can move in with you. Do you have a barn or somewhere you can practice nearby?"

She didn't bother to hide the sigh rumbling against her ribs. She stared at the dilapidated old barn that had deteriorated since her father's death. Her Mom and sister hadn't the heart or inclination to keep ranching after he had passed on, and they had sold off all the stock except for her sister's horse and a few chickens. They had a mess of barn cats that seemed to triple every time she visited. "No. No barn. Nowhere to practice here. Not enough room to host the band. It's just a small family home. Besides, my mother needs quiet and rest." *Did she have to start spelling things out to Roger, too? Were her words coming out so mumbled that no one understood her lately? Or were all men morons?*

"Bummer. Any big hotels nearby? A mansion to rent for a couple months?"

"This isn't L.A. where there's a plethora of mansions for rent. Nor am I a real estate agent. See what you can arrange and get back to me. And remember, only call me Wendy."

"You giving another poor sap the Wendy speech? W-e-n-d-y." Trace sauntered into the living room as if he owned the joint.

She jumped, her eyes so wide her cheeks hurt. She covered the mouthpiece of the phone with her hand. "What are you doing here?"

"I've always come over here. Remember? Well, maybe not, as you hardly seem to remember this is your home." Trace towered over her, blocking the window's view.

She whispered into the phone. "Just do your job and call me when you have news for me." When Roger started to protest, she cut him off and powered off her phone so he couldn't call back and pester her. She could only deal with one troublesome man at a time, and Trace counted double already.

"What do you want?"

"Is that your best bedside manner?" Challenge lit his eyes, and he flexed his muscles as though he was showing off.

"I'm not a physician. I don't have to have a bedside manner. I live in this house and as far as I know, you're trespassing. Goodbye." She strode to the kitchen for a glass of water to cool her parched throat. She groaned when he followed her. "What part of goodbye don't you understand?"

"This is practically my house. I never needed an invitation to come in before."

Was he trying to tell her something? Okay. She'd bite. "So, is this your way of telling me you're engaged to my sister? Or did we finally adopt you?"

Without blinking an eyelash, he pulled up a chair and straddled it backwards. "You adopted me, yourself, years ago."

The man was absolutely incorrigible. Even in the music industry, few had thicker hides. "Me?" She stuck out her lower lip and shook her head. "I think I'd remember adopting a grown man."

Unofficially, she had taken Thunder and Lightning under her wing, but she wasn't about to mention that. He'd tease her till the day she died, not to mention the barrage of questions it would bring about her personal life.

"Your family. I ate more of your mother's cooking than my own mom's."

She snapped her fingers and whirled on him. "I remember! You were the family pet, waiting for us to throw you table scraps." In accordance with her words, she made an extra peanut butter and banana sandwich and poured two glasses of milk. She slid them down the counter to him, then took a bite of her own. *This was food of the Gods. If she was trapped on a deserted island for the rest of her life and could only have one meal, this would be it.*

"I see you didn't inherit your mother's culinary expertise." He sunk his teeth deep into the sandwich and swallowed the mouthful in one big gulp.

She wanted a snack, and he leaped to the conclusion that she couldn't cook? Oy! She strode over to him, yanked the sandwich from his hands and tossed it down the garbage disposal. Her appetite had dried up too, so her sandwich followed. "Make your own food, then. Wendy's kitchen is closed—permanently."

Trace jumped to his feet, knocking the chair over. "Whoa, Freddie. What's eating you? Still can't take a little good natured teasing?" He licked a glob of peanut butter off his lips, drawing her attention to his tongue.

Good, strong tongue. It looked like he could flick it better than Lightning. How much practice did he have using that tongue...

She shook herself, furious that she still fantasized about any part of him. She was an adult now, years out of high school. And Trace had made it ultra clear that he found her sister much more to his liking. So, why did he insist on following Wendy around now? Her insults would have withered a normal man hours ago.

His arm shot out, blocking her exit from the kitchen when she tried to stalk out.

Okay. So, he demanded an answer. "You. You're eating me. No one calls me Freddie but you. And no one else has ever insulted my peanut butter and banana sandwiches." She couldn't bring herself to admit that his tongue, his scent, his mere presence disturbed her, and made her want to run back to L.A. with her heart still intact.

When a lascivious look flickered across his eyes, she realized her faux pas. "Of course, I don't mean you're literally eating me. I meant you bother me…" A frustrated cry tore from her lips.

The devil chuckled. *How dare he laugh at her, on top of calling her Freddie!* "How do I bother you? Was that a Freudian slip? Do you want me to eat you?" He flicked his tongue out at her as his gaze roamed her length and settled on the juncture of her thighs.

Latent desire exploded in her, making her quiver. If she didn't escape this second, she was going to do something embarrassing, like drool or drag him to her bedroom, which still contained all the sickening juvenile pink lace and girly belongings. "I can't believe you said that. Back, demon."

"You're the one dressed all in black like a vampire. When did you go goth? I never figured you for the type."

Sighing, she ducked under his arm and torpedoed to the pink cave. "Go doctor your real patient and stop psychoanalyzing me. Shoo!"

"Who are you, and what did you do with our Freddie?" His hot breath tickled her neck as he whispered huskily in her ear.

Infuriated by the constant use of her dreaded nickname, she gritted her teeth. "There never was a Freddie." She slammed her door, locked it, and leaned against it. She sank to the floor and buried her face in her hands.

* * * * *

Wendy awoke with a start. The door shook and a picture fell off her wall and shattered. People yelled.

"Earthquake!" She tucked her head between her knees and covered it with her arms. Then she remembered she was in Florida, not California. Florida suffered from hurricanes, not earthquakes, and although hurricanes could rattle a house, too, Doppler weather gave advance warning.

"Wendy! You in there? Or did you run away again?" Angel didn't sound particularly angelic.

Wendy sighed and scrambled to her feet. She yawned widely and rubbed the sleep from her eyes. "I'm coming! Stop beating down the door, would ya?"

She unlocked the door and opened it to her sister, who glared at her. "What do you want?"

Angel stepped gingerly over the broken glass from the frame she had caused to fall from the wall, and regarded her with hostility. "Some help, for one. You've hardly seen Mama since you flew in."

"Jet lag must've caught up with me." She hadn't slept in almost forty-eight hours. No wonder she'd crashed.

Angel's gaze raked the made-up bed. "Where'd you sleep? In the chair?"

"On the floor." Wendy knelt and picked up shards of glass.

"Trace is right. You are acting strangely. What gives?" Angel circled her as if swooping in for the kill.

"Nothing," she lied, trying to smile and failing. *She was only lying to her family, her fans…the world.* Juggling the lies was difficult enough in L.A. when her family was a thousand miles away and not watching her under a microscope. It was going to be darn near impossible to keep her secret under their noses.

"Well, I have a beauty contest, and I need your help. I'll be away for a few days." Angelina lifted her nose in the air and flicked her hair behind her shoulder.

The Orlando gig was coming up and she didn't know the rest of her schedule, yet. "What days? I have some engagements I can't cancel." The glass tinkled when she dropped it in the garbage can, and she bounced on her haunches.

"What do you mean, you can't take over? I thought that's why you came home." Angel's voice was so sharp, it sliced through Wendy, and she winced.

"I came home to help and to be with Mom through her recovery, but I wasn't able to get out of all my commitments." Wendy tried to practice patience as she smoothed the ruined certificate.

"You mean you're irreplaceable? No one else can sell your feminine hygiene products?"

Wendy's hackles rose. As usual, her life and job were unimportant to her sister. Angel's disdain really irked her, but she knew she had caused some of the problem by spinning the lies in the first place. Still, if she had a regular job like a sales person, should that be any less important than Angel's career? "We have to make a schedule. Maybe we need to hire another nurse that can be here when we can't."

"But I need someone to help me at the pageant! Mama's always helped me. I was counting on you." Angel stared up at the moon, her reflection in the window drawn and morose. And yet, with the moonlight highlighting her glossy shoulder-length hair, she looked angelic, like her name.

Wendy gulped, wanting to retch. Indigestion rose in her chest, coating her throat. The old phobias about her sister's beauty contests, rushed in on her, and her hands grew clammy. Unlike when she was a kid and wished Angel would trip and fall off the stage, she wished her well. But she didn't have the time to baby-sit her. She had concerts to play and practices with the band. "I really can't promise till I know your pageant dates and my own schedule."

"So, you won't support me. Fine! I should've known you wouldn't. You haven't been there for me in years." Angel huffed off, her skirts swirling about her ankles.

Wishing she had a closer relationship with her only sibling, she swallowed a sigh as she watched her departure. Maybe it was her fault, at least partially, for not showing more interest in her sister's dream. Did it matter that she couldn't stomach the fawning over all the beautiful, brainless Barbie dolls that pranced and paraded around the pageants like goddesses? Who looked down their noses and laughed at ugly trolls like herself? She was an adult now and could handle herself. Couldn't she?

She chewed her lower lip, pondering if she should go after her sister and try to make amends. But how? She couldn't give her what she wanted, to skip Orlando.

Her cell phone trilled in her pocket. She sighed and grabbed it. "Aloha."

"Got good news for you, duckie. We rented a house, and Storm is on their way now. Write down this address." Roger's enthusiasm vibrated through the line, defying the static interference.

"Give me a sec to get paper and pen." She rifled through the vanity drawers until she found a piece of her old stationery, a romantic design with embossed shells and lace on pink parchment. She wrote down the address, glowering that it was as near as the neighboring town.

"Do you have our new schedule yet?" She hugged the phone between her ear and her shoulder as she paced the room, fingering pieces of her childhood.

"Not all of it, but write these dates down."

She scribbled Miami, Ft. Lauderdale, West Palm Beach, Tampa, Key West, Naples, Tallahassee, Jacksonville, Atlanta, and Mobile. She frowned at the last two. "Rog, I really can't travel far."

"That's why planes were invented. Zip, zip, and you'll be there. It's the best I could do on such short notice. And your fans on the West Coast are not happy with you. You'll have to do some major groveling to get back in their good graces."

"Can we give them a free or reduced concert when I can go back on tour? For the ticket holders of the canceled shows, I mean." She gazed out at the twinkling stars. She'd forgotten how beautiful the Florida night sky was. The fantastic view mesmerized her.

"And are you going to pay the promoters and fees? Not one of your brighter ideas."

She scowled at the phone. "So, when will Storm be here?"

A floorboard creaked, and she whirled around, aghast to find Trace lounging against her open door's frame. His shadow mingled with hers, like lovers.

Oh, dear God! What if he'd heard her? Her blood froze in her veins, and she became petrified for several seconds, unable to even exhale. Trace couldn't find out. He was the real reason she'd insisted on the elaborate disguises. For years, she'd longed for him to look past her outer layer to the person within, and he hadn't. If someday he began to like her…or fell in love with her…she wanted it to be for herself, not her exciting, glamorous alter ego.

"You there, duckie?" Roger banged the phone several times against a hard object, waking her out of her stupor, propelling her into action.

"Oh? A bad storm's coming? Okay, we'll take precautions. Thanks!" She flipped the phone shut in the middle of Roger's rant. She turned off the pesky device and hid it in her pocket.

Trace brushed past her and stared out her window at the clear sky. "Storm? There's not a cloud in sight."

"Oh, it's coming all right," she muttered under her breath. *Both the band and the nuclear holocaust if and when her family found out about her secret identity.*

His silhouette was framed by the window. Tall, muscular, and majestic, with a silvery sheen compliments of the moonlight, he was so beautiful that he stole her breath. It wasn't fair for a man to be so gorgeous when she was so plain. Angry with herself for such fanciful musings, she terminated her thoughts. "And why do I have the honor of your company again?" She bit off 'in my boudoir' in the nick of time. She didn't want to be accused of more Freudian slips.

"Your mother's awake and asking for you." His gaze raked over her, as if he found nothing of interest to linger on.

Pain swelled in her heart, and she turned away. He'd never look at Angel like that. Hurting, she snapped, "Why are you still here so late? Don't you ever go home?"

"I take my job seriously. Plus, Bessie's a friend." He dogged her steps to her mother's bedside, smelling of an evergreen forest after a rain shower. She cursed her olfactory senses, knowing they should be ruined after so much time spent in smoky coliseums. The man had no right to smell so wonderful.

A gray cast had settled over her mother's porcelain features, tugging at Wendy's heart. Her mother was normally so tough, so feisty, this frail version scared her. Maybe Trace was too optimistic about her condition. Maybe she should get a second opinion.

Bessie's lashes fluttered and fell as if she didn't have the strength to open her eyes. She flexed her gnarled fingers. "Is that you, Wenefred?"

Wendy curled her fingers around her mother's and tried not to strangle on her words. "Yes. It's me, Mom."

Her mother managed to prop open one eye and pinned her with a reproachful gaze. "What's this, I hear, that you won't help Angelina with her pageant? I know you were always green with envy as a little girl, but you're a grown woman now. It's not a pretty sight."

Funny, she still felt like that pushed-aside, unloved little girl. But her mother was right. She was a woman now. A woman with a career that was far more important than her sister's bimbos on parade.

She took a deep breath, preparing her defense. "I am grown up. And it's not that I don't want to support Angel, it's just that I have my own job and it requires my attention."

Bessie snorted and narrowed her eyes. "Pshaw! You can't tell me that you can't take a sabbatical or even quit that dime-a-dozen job until I'm out of the woods. I need you to fill in for me, and that means going with Angelina to her pageants."

Now Wendy remembered why she'd run like hell away from here. Her job, her life, meant nothing to her family. *Quit her dime-a-dozen job.* Hyperventilating, she forced herself to take deep breaths.

Of course, her mother didn't know the truth. It was confession time. Her blood drained from her face, and dizziness assailed her. Nausea attacked her stomach. "Trace, could I have a moment alone with my mom? I need to tell her something."

"Tell me what?" Bessie shot up in her bed, the covers bunching around her waist. Her graying hair hung in straggly clumps, and her bedclothes were badly rumpled.

Trace clasped Wendy's elbow and applied pressure. Electric current sizzled up her arm and gave her a jolt. His warm breath on her neck started a series of mini earthquakes in the pit of her stomach. "Careful what you say to her. She's not strong enough for arguments or deep dark confessions."

"Excuse us a moment, Bessie," Trace said louder. He escorted Wendy from the room and closed the door behind them. "Tell me first what you plan to say to her."

Bristling, she yanked away from him. "I beg your pardon, but it was private for her ears only." *Trace was the last person on Earth she wanted to know her secret.*

He folded his arms over his impressive chest and squared his shoulders, towering over her. "Either you tell me first and let me judge if she can handle it, or you keep your mouth shut till she's fully recovered."

Boiling, she tried to leash her fury. Waiting until after her mother was better wouldn't resolve the problem now. "So, what do you suggest, Doctor?"

He plunged his hands deep into his pockets and rocked back on his heels. "Pacify her. Go along with what she wants. Would it kill you to support your sister this one time?"

His proverbial slap almost knocked her backwards. "What about me? I have an important job, too, and I can't just slough it off. I'm not asking anyone to quit their job to support me, just for a little consideration to let me do what I have to do."

Trace scowled at her and he stopped rocking. "Help me understand. It's not as if no one can fill in for you, or as if someone will die…"

That was it! She couldn't take it any more. "Oh, since I'm not a big, important doctor like you, my job doesn't matter? Well, it matters to me." *And to a lot of other people.* She wanted to scream or hit something, and her hands fisted at her sides.

"And what about your mother? Does she matter to you?"

His question wrapped her in guilt, diffusing her anger. *Did he think her so low? So inhuman? So selfish?* The weight of her mother's and the band's future crushed in on her. She wished she was just plain, unimportant Wendy so she wouldn't have these huge problems. Temporarily defeated, she released a sigh. "Okay, you win. I'll wait till Mom's better to tell her." But she didn't feel relieved, just the opposite.

* * * * *

Freddie puzzled him. When had her heart shriveled, and why? What was she hiding? If it was something that could hurt his patient, he needed to know. She looked like a volcano ready to erupt. And he had a bad feeling the fallout would be a bitch.

What huge secret could she be hiding? Maybe she wasn't selling feminine hygiene products. Maybe she was an international spy selling arms or government secrets? Or maybe she was married and had kids and a husband squirreled away and waiting for her to return home.

He dismissed the second possibility. Why would she hide a husband from her mother and sister? Why not tell him? Maybe she was a lesbian?

No. He didn't think that possible, either, although she was a lot more assertive and volatile than he recalled.

He dropped his hands to her shoulders and spoke next to her ear. "What big secret are you keeping? You can tell me. We're long time buddies."

She tensed and glared up at him. Fireworks sparked in her eyes, and she looked more beautifully intense than ever before. "Buddies? I've not heard from you in at least five years. Some buddy." She closed the door in his face.

He narrowed his eyes. She hadn't refuted hiding a secret, but she hadn't given him any clues as to what it might be, either. He opened the door and followed her into the room to make sure she followed orders, and was hit with an arctic blast of anger from her. She'd gone psycho when he said they'd been buddies and offered a confiding ear. *Why?*

Freddie was hiding something. As both her mother's attending physician and long time friend, he wanted to know what. She warranted close monitoring and a little investigation.

Chapter Three

Sneaking off to Palm Lakes for an afternoon or late at night wasn't too difficult. Traipsing off to Orlando for the weekend was another matter.

"You can't just pick up and leave me alone with Mama." Angel followed Wendy around munching on a carrot stick, which seemed to comprise her entire lunch. She smacked her lips like a cow, annoying Wendy.

Chuckling without mirth she said, "You make it sound like I'm staging a mutiny. I'll be back Monday morning. You were planning for both of us to be gone for your pageant next week. Isn't that worse?"

"The nurse'll be here with her..."

"Precisely. Just as she is now. You have my cell number. Call if there's an emergency, and I'll come right back."

"If it's that easy, don't go." Angel thrust her chin out and struck a regal stance.

"Then don't go to your pageant, either." *It sounded fair to her. Well, not quite.* She had a contract and an obligation to perform this concert. It was her career. Her life. What was a beauty pageant in comparison? It was time that her sister grew up and pursued a real career. She couldn't be a beauty queen forever.

"Oh, you're totally insufferable. You're just jealous like Mama said. You can't stand it that I was the favorite. *Nobody loves me, everybody hates me.* Wasn't that your mantra? Poor, poor, Wendy. I was always supposed to feel sorry for you. Well, I'm tired of feeling sorry for you."

Wendy sank to her bed. *Is that how her sister saw her? Not merely ugly, but pathetic? Whiny? Impossibly jealous? Could that be true?*

Even if it was, she had to go to Orlando. Roger would send a posse for her if she even thought of canceling. He'd dig her up from the grave if she dared to die.

Should she tell her sister the truth? Almost as soon as the thought crossed her mind, she banished it. Angel couldn't keep a secret. She'd tell their mother…and Trace…before she could blink. So, she was stuck suffering her sister's wrath.

"I have to go. That's final." Wendy rolled up her clothes and packed them, a trick she'd learned from her sister's pageants. It was the only thing of value she'd taken from the beauty contests.

Angel flounced to the door, her nostrils flaring and her cheeks flushed. "Fine. Don't expect me to help you when you need a favor."

Wendy rolled her eyes mentally. "Whatever." When had Angel ever been there for her? As long as she could remember, her activities had been put on hold for Angel's pursuit of one crown after another. Even the singing audition she'd had to miss when she was seventeen. That still stung like crazy.

Storm was more of a loving, supportive family than her own sister had ever been. And that included Roger, the control freak.

But as much as she tried to put it out of her mind, her sister's words plagued her during the entire flight to Orlando.

Panting for air, Roger rushed to meet her at the Orlando terminal. "I was afraid you'd stand us up, duckie."

She shot her manager a withering smile and then softened, and hugged him. "It's good to see you, too, Rog."

She tucked her arm through his as he led her to their hired car. He'd shaved his dark hair close to his head and a diamond stud in his ear winked in the light. The crowd jostled them, so that her overnight bag slapped her side.

"You've not damaged your million dollar pipes calling to the piggies on your farm, have you?" He held the Mercedes' door wide for her and then slid into the seat beside her.

Slightly insulted at his insinuation that her small hometown was akin to living at Green Acres, she screwed up her lips and punched him playfully on the shoulder. He was a city slicker, through and through, and probably thought that Florida was one large, swampy alligator ranch. "We have no piggies, thank you very much. The only danger to my voice comes from screeching at my sister."

"You didn't, did you?" Alarm flashed across his thin, ruddy face.

"No. But if anyone could tempt me, it would be her." *Or Trace.*

Roger offered her a piece of gum. When she shook her head, he popped a piece in his mouth. He needed it to help him kick his cigarette habit. She was afraid of damaging her teeth or doing anything that could adversely affect her ability to sing.

Orlando traffic was a bear, but the scenery was exciting. A fantasy world, they passed theme parks, roller coasters, King Kong-sized apes, pagodas, and about a million tourists wearing flowered Hawaiian shirts and straw hats, threading their way in and out of palm tree-studded sidewalks. The city had really grown since her last visit.

When they reached their hotel, a five-star, multi-storied, glass tower, Thunder waited for them at the curb. Firm, sexy lips crooked into a devilish smile as he folded her into a clinch and planted a hard kiss on her lips. After she regained her balance, she shook her head. "Need I remind you that you're married?"

Thunder grimaced and took her bag. "I really wish you'd stop reminding me." Even out of costume, he was a sight to behold, long, blond, wavy hair cascaded down to one of the best-sculpted asses in the world. Sapphire eyes glowed with appreciation and mischief, a much prettier color than the grassy green contacts he wore while in makeup. Although not as classically beautiful as Trace, his masculine features were chiseled and compelling.

"Well, someone obviously has to." She hoped Thunder was teasing. An incurable flirt, he couldn't help but admire and compliment women. Not that it was an entirely horrible trait, but not one she wanted in her future husband. She should thank Carly for saving her from such a fate. He knew how to charm her and sneak under her guard, and she still felt a lot of affection for him.

"Carly remembers well enough for both of us." His frown was comical and Wendy burst out laughing.

"You could save yourself the room fee and bunk with me," Thunder whispered in her ear and had the audacity to lick it.

Shocked, she jumped back. This was brazen, even for Thunder. "Look, I don't want any crazed, jealous wives gunning for me. I'm here for a concert, not a horror show." Besides, although his wet tongue shocked her, it didn't excite her as it once had.

"If you change your mind, I'm in the adjoining room. There's a connecting door..." He ran his fingertip down the length of her arm and licked his lips.

"Peachy." *Not!* Maybe she'd sneak down later and switch rooms. Maybe even floors.

Roger tsk-tsked and stepped between them. "No time for flirting now. Put your cases in the room and meet me out front in ten."

"Slave driver," Thunder muttered under his breath. "He sucks the fun out of everything."

"Ian, come with me, and please stop your bitching and moaning before you give me another migraine. Wendy's a big girl and doesn't need your help to freshen up." Roger cut between them like a sheep dog and corralled Thunder away from her.

She shot Roger a grateful look, but wondered what to do about Thunder's increasingly blatant advances? Maybe Rain would share a room with her from now on, and act as a quasi-chaperone. Although knowing the incorrigible guitarist, he'd merely suggest a threesome.

Unfortunately, Rain liked to bring groupies back to her room after the concerts. Wendy shivered. One of them could be Jack the Ripper and they wouldn't know till it was too late. *Nix that idea.*

Within moments, she was caught up in the fanfare of the concert. She slipped into her Skye Blue persona with ease. For a few blissful hours, she forgot Wendy

Applegate's existence. Unfettered by her daily bonds, the music rocked through her. She sang, flung her hair about her head wildly, and pranced onstage, making love to her microphone and her audience.

The lights were hellishly hot, beating down and blinding her. Perspiration trickled down her back.

She sang a duet with Thunder, their lips within kissing distance, their breath mingling. As the last notes of their song faded, the audience roared and whistled.

When she turned to the audience to accept their praise, something abnormal caught her attention. Decked in black leather and spikes, sandy blonde hair slicked back, and with chest bared stood the one person in the world she never would have expected to see. It couldn't be. It wasn't possible. *Trace?* Could this punked out rocker really be the respectable doctor?

Her mouth went dry, and she froze, her gaze glued to the vision in leather. He must be a look-alike. Trace would never dress in black leather or chains. He wasn't that cool. Yet she couldn't catch her breath or remember what to do next.

Thunder pulled her up. "Snap out of it, Skye."

She tore her gaze from the Trace look-alike, still in a daze. "I'm cool," she lied, and followed Thunder in a rehearsed dance across stage.

Throughout the rest of the concert, she kept sneaking glances at the hunk, wondering if he could be Trace. If it was, what was he doing here? She'd never seen him at a Storm performance before. Nor was she aware that he liked her kind of music.

Finally, the concert ended in a symphony of light. The band got called back for two curtain calls and performed their final bow, hand in hand. Mr. Leather disappeared by the final set. A mixture of relief and disappointment overcame her.

Thunder and Lightning carried her offstage. But this time was different. The Trace clone stood next to the local radio DJ, with a group of listeners who had won backstage passes to meet Storm. He smiled and winked, completely bewitching her.

Astonished, she couldn't flutter an eyelash. She shivered, but whatever the culprit, the chilly air conditioning whooshing over her perspiration-drenched clothes, or the man's intent gaze raking her body, she wasn't sure.

Everyone else faded into the background as the man swallowed up the space between them. "Hi," he murmured huskily. The rich timbre of Trace's voice washed over her, and she blinked.

"Hi," she murmured back, and froze, afraid he'd recognize her voice. She was grateful for the crowd's ruckus so that he couldn't hear her clearly. At least she hoped he couldn't. But she couldn't voice another word to him. She had to escape but her knees had turned to jelly.

"You're even more beautiful up close." Trace smiled down at her, his lips utterly dreamy and kissable.

She started to croak, "I am?" then remembered her own resolve not to talk. Playing charades, she pointed to her throat and then waved her finger at him.

"You can't talk? You have a sore throat?"

She nodded, grasping for any excuse to avoid him. She pointed to her dressing room, shrugged, and started to back away. She waved goodbye.

But he followed her, undeterred. "I'm a doctor. I could take a look at it and make sure you're not coming down with something."

She had to smile at that. No one had ever looked less like a doctor than he did at this moment. She let her gaze sweep him slowly, lingering on his exceptional assets well delineated by the tight black leather britches molding his body. It was one of the many privileges Skye enjoyed which Wendy dared not. Skye was a brazen hussy, or so the tabloids reported. Wendy was a prude. Being a hussy had definite advantages.

He chuckled wickedly and leaned over her proprietarily. "I know. I don't look like a doctor right now, but I am. I promise I don't bite."

She wasn't so sure about that, but decided she might just enjoy being nibbled by him very much. She crooked her finger at him and he followed her into the room. She sat on the overstuffed couch and patted the seat beside her. He smelled of leather, smoke, and…*beer?*

When he sat down, she opened her mouth wide and he shined a penlight down her throat, his warm breath tickling her face, his lips mere kissing distance away. "You look perfect to me. I guess your throat is just a little strained from the workout."

Awed by his compliment, her heart fluttered. She didn't know whether to wriggle out from beneath him or wrap her legs around him and ravish his sexy body here and now.

He delved his fingers through her hair. "Why do you wear this disguise? Is it to drive men wild?"

She gulped, and nodded. Then, deciding to be Skye and not Wendy tonight, she put her lips to his and stole a kiss. She might never get another chance. Trace would never let Wendy the troll kiss him. He tasted so good, and she felt so wonderful, she moaned in his mouth.

He growled and pushed her back against the couch. She didn't know whether to wriggle out from beneath him or wrap her legs around him and ravish his sexy body here and now. He drank deeply of her until they tore apart for air. Gasping for breath, she rubbed her palms down his chest, and then up over his magnificently muscled arms.

If he weren't so hot and pliant, he could be a statue, he was so well-honed. She couldn't wait to see the rest of him. Since this would be her only chance to taste him, to be one body and soul, she took it.

Moaning, she ran her tongue along the curve of his neck, where she knew she was most sensitive. He tasted so good, salty and musky, and she moaned her pleasure.

He laced his fingers in her hair, holding her head.

She nibbled his nipples, then swirled them with her tongue. They puckered in her mouth, and he arched his back. His groin swelled, pressing against her stomach. It felt enormous, and she wanted to know if it matched the rest of his physique.

When his hand cupped her breast, her panic warred with her white-hot desire. As he kneaded her nipple hypnotically, desire won out. Wildfire scorched her veins and lava bubbled in her core. She was about to go up in flames. Writhing beneath him, her panic subsiding, she licked a trail of fire down his chest, and flicked her tongue across his navel.

Power surged through her when he moaned and flexed his cock. Sliding her hands inside his pants, she massaged firm buttocks. Exquisitely sculpted, they were tight and firm.

"You're as wild as all the reports." He panted between each word, his breathing ragged. "And even hotter."

She wasn't about to disavow him of his fantasy and tell him this was one of her rare walks on the wild side. She wasn't going to say anything to douse his fire.

She wanted to stoke him, make him rage out of control until he ravished her. She wanted to feel his possession every place she could and then start all over. This would be their only night together, and she wanted a treasury of memories to last her a lifetime.

His hair teased her, trickling from his navel and disappearing under his pants. Starving, she nibbled her way down his rock hard abs. A deliciously wicked idea teased her mind. Wild women turned him on. She growled and ripped open his pants. The sound of the snap exploded in her ears, the only other sound was their heavy, erratic breathing.

Reverently, she sat on her knees between his legs, unzipped his slacks, and then worked them down his legs. Awed by his velvety hardness, she sucked in her breath.

He was so beautiful, so thick and dark red with desire. She swallowed hard as she cupped his balls in one hand and wrapped her fingers around his pulsing shaft. His cock had turned granite hard.

Pre-cum beaded on the tip, and she rubbed the pad of her thumb over it and then down the long length, making it slicker. She couldn't believe she was being intimate with the love of her life, that he was in her dressing room naked, primed to make her his. She prayed this wasn't a dream and if it was, that she'd never awaken.

When he tried to sit up, she pushed him back down and shook her finger at him. She wasn't done with him yet, and he wasn't going to preempt her wickedly seductive plans.

Juices flowed between her legs as she nestled her head between his thighs. She flicked her tongue over the head of his penis and tasted his sap.

His fingers tangled deeper into her tresses and dragged her head down.

Opening her lips wide, she took him into her mouth as deeply as she could. She caressed his cock, and fluffed his wiry curls. She loved making him shiver and writhe. When he began to pump into her mouth, she slid her lips off, centimeter by scrumptious centimeter.

He groaned in protest and tried to hold her head in place as he started to buck.

But she wanted him buried deep inside her the first time he spewed his seed, so she shook her head and drew herself to her feet. Wanting to give him a private performance he would never forget, she stripped for him, slowly, seductively. She skimmed her palms down her breasts and then unsnapped her halter and let it slide off her arms to puddle at her feet.

His intense gaze stoked her fire, and she rubbed her nipples till they peaked. Languorously, she drew her hands down her flat stomach and slid her fingers under the stretch waistband of her mini skirt. She swayed her hips forward as if fucking him, all the while tracing her lips with the tip of her tongue, savoring his sweet ambrosia that still lingered on them.

Slowly, she pushed down her skirt and then her G-string, revealing her Brazilian wax job. Then, in case his ardor was cooling, and to prepare herself, she slid her index finger into her pussy and stroked in and out as his eyes smoldered passionately, growing wide as headlights.

"Get on me, woman, before I come all over myself," he growled and pumped his cock.

Tossing him an impish smile, she rubbed her swollen, aching nipples over his wet rod. Rising higher, she molded her chest to his. She laughed and the silvery tinkle washed over her to be smothered a second later with his intoxicating kiss.

His fingers massaged her nipples, and his cock flexed against her naked, ultra-sensitized labia, making her squirm.

Tearing her lips from his, she straddled him. His strong heart pounded under her hands and she reveled in his power. She let him part her lips and plunge deep into her core.

Rapturous waves flooded her. His thrusts were swift and deep, as he stretched her vaginal walls with his amazing girth. Squeezing her eyes shut, she flung her head back so that her loosened hair splayed across her flesh. Wild as the wind, she rode him hard, milking his seed.

His thighs corded as he thrust into her one final time. She ground her hips on his, his coarse hair tickling her, until her release came. Their juices mixed and spilled out, coating her legs.

He cradled her to his chest, stroked her hair, and kissed her tenderly. When he surfaced, he mumbled against her mouth, "That was incredible."

She smiled softly and nodded, snuggling against him. His heart raced next to her ear and she kissed him, flaming their smoldering fire.

Trace growled and flipped her over on her stomach. When her heavy breasts swung freely, and her nipples grazed the leather of the couch, she shivered.

"You like that," Trace muttered, his smoky velvet voice washing over her. He rose to his full stature, towering over her.

Her heart flip-flopped as she scrambled to her knees. Her heavy breasts swung freely and her nipples grazed the leather and she shivered.

His large hands gripped her hips, and he teased her with the tip of his penis. *How excruciatingly torturous.*

Her nerve endings screaming, she wriggled against it, starved for its possession. She smiled secretively that he could be such a tease. She'd never suspected this side of him, but she loved it. Still, she was about to murder him if he didn't hurry up and give it to her.

"You want it bad." It wasn't a question.

Duh! She growled and ground her ass against the sole object of her desire.

"You ready for that ménage a trois, luv?" Thunder's sultry voice sent shock waves through her.

Appalled at being caught naked in the act of making love, she started to scream at him to get out. The notes choked in her throat when she sobered enough to remember that Trace might recognize her voice.

She yearned to wipe the smug smile from Thunder's face, so she did the next best thing—glowering, she flung her spiky heel at his head with all her might. Her aim wicked, the deadly projectile flew true. But the lithe musician was too agile and ducked a split second before it found its mark and torpedoed into the wall behind him.

Chapter Four

Wendy breathed a sigh of relief when she reached her rental car, a shiny black sports coup complete with automatic transmission and a sunroof. She had been scared that someone would lay in wait for her, but her fears were unfounded. No one accosted her in the hall, and the moon-dappled parking lot was deserted.

As she fumbled with her keys, a long shadow fell across hers. A distorted reflection slid along the chrome.

Whirling around, she gasped, her heart beating louder than Rain's drums. *Shouldn't she have heard something to alert her to another presence? A footstep crunching the gravel? Heavy breathing?* Creepy, villainous music like in B-rated horror flicks? A tall, lithe man towered over her, his face hidden by darkness. He could be Thunder or Trace...or a total stranger. She stepped back and was trapped against her car. "Who are you? What do you want?"

Thunder stepped into the dim circle of light cast by a nearby street lamp. His hair was pulled back in a hair tie, and he wore all black, which explained his invisibility. "Who was that?"

She blinked. What right did he have to know? He wasn't her husband, and they hadn't been lovers for years. "Just a fan."

Thunder leaned on her car, preventing her from opening the door. "You don't sleep around, especially not with fans."

Heat rushed into her cheeks, but she hoped the dark clouds overhead would cover her discomfort. Thunder knew her too well. He was right. He didn't have to know that. "I made an exception. Women get horny, too. He lit my fire."

"Now, you sound like a bad version of that Jim Morrison song. So, why didn't you call me? I'd have taken care of your needs." He invaded her comfort zone, so close his hot breath scorched her forehead.

Her gaze drifted to his shiny gold wedding band that refracted moonlight. She grabbed his hand and lifted it to his face. "See this? That's why." Well, that wasn't the only reason, but it was all the reason he needed to know. Just as she didn't want anyone to know about Storm and her part in it, she didn't want Storm to know about Trace.

"How do you know the guy that was banging you isn't hitched?" Challenge oozed from him.

"He wasn't wearing a wedding ring."

Thunder snorted. "Most married men don't. That proves nothing."

Annoyed by this inquisition, she shook her head. Exhaustion claimed her, mentally, physically, and spiritually. It was as if all the oxygen had fled her brain, and she felt woozy. She wasn't up to a game of twenty questions when all she wanted to do was soak in a nice warm bubble bath. "I just know, okay? Can I go home now? I'm ready to collapse."

Thunder snapped his fingers in front of her eyes. "You know him! You're too anal to screw a stranger."

Insulted, she thrust out her chest. Since when was she anal? "This is ridiculous. Are you going to let me get in my car so I can go back to the hotel? Or are you going to cross-examine me till dawn?"

"So, who is he?"

She wasn't a prisoner of war or a criminal, so she wasn't even going to give him her name, rank, and serial number. "Bite me."

Mischief rolled across Thunder's eyes. "Love to. Thought you'd never ask. I know just where I want to start."

She rolled her eyes. His immaturity usually both annoyed and amused her. Today, he did not amuse her. "Grow up." She gazed longingly at the seats. She was so tired, she could just curl up on one and snooze right here.

"I'm just watching out for you."

"I can watch out for myself, thank you very much." She was a big girl now. She could handle whatever life tossed at her.

He finally moved, and she climbed back into the car. What a bad scene! But it could've been worse. What if Trace had followed her instead?

* * * * *

Trace walked around in a daze. He'd just lived his dream—to make love to the beautiful singer, Skye Blue. When he'd dressed in that leather getup, he'd never imagined for a moment that she'd see him among the crowd, much less favor him with her kisses and give him her body.

She had a wild reputation, but still he hadn't expected a band member to barge in on them and suggest a ménage a trois. Did she engage in threesomes often?

He had hoped to get her out of his system. A grown professional man should not have a raging thing for a rock idol. But instead of purging her from his mind and heart, his lust for her was a hundred times stronger. And he hadn't even seen her face. What if she was a dog under that grease paint? Did that matter? She had one hard body, and a luscious voice. And her kisses made his cock hard.

It flexed and stiffened as he thought about the songstress. Not good. He was on duty, and his neighbors wouldn't understand his deviant behavior of Saturday night. He arranged his doctor's jacket to hide his arousal.

"Am I going to live, Doc?" Bessie struggled to sit up and rolled her gown sleeve down where he had just finished taking her blood pressure.

At least she hadn't called him kid. He wrote down her vital signs and then peered at her. "If you get that blood pressure down and stop getting so upset about everything. I'm going to give you a prescription for it."

She waved him off. "You know I hate drugs. Can't remember to take them. All the medicine I need is to have my girls here and for them to get along."

"Dream on, Mom." Freddie had entered midway through Bessie's statement, and butted in where she wasn't welcome or needed. "You know Angel lives to torture me."

"See? She's trying to push me into an early grave. Tell her it's a matter of life and death that she should be nice to me." Bessie glared at her eldest daughter.

"What am I being blamed for this time?" Freddie stopped in her tracks, stiffening. Her dark brows drew together, and she looked from her mother to him and back.

Trace gave her his most stern physician's look, hoping she'd cooperate for her mother's sake. It wouldn't hurt her to instill some peace and harmony in her home, either. Or to make amends with her sister. "I was just telling your mother that her blood pressure is too high, and I prescribed some medicine for it. But she also needs calm and quiet. That's where you and Angelina come in. I need you to promise me that you won't do anything to upset your mother."

Freddie gulped and forced a smile to her lips, which didn't reach her eyes. "Anything to help Mom get well."

"I hope you mean that, Missy. What would make me happy is if you settle down here, get married, and start giving me some grandchildren before I'm gone and never get to meet them." Bessie slid a sly glance at him and tilted her head. "The good doctor here is still single. He needs a wife."

Trace almost choked and had to turn away. Settling down wasn't in his plans. He still had years ahead of him before he had to succumb to marriage.

Freddie sighed audibly, causing him to turn back. "Well, yeah, I see how much he loves the thought. I'll visit when you're through with your checkup. Ring the bell if you need anything." With that, she pivoted on her heel and walked out.

Trace felt like a bastard. She had obviously taken his reaction the wrong way. For as long as he'd known Freddie, she had been very self-effacing and down on herself. She had seemed surer of herself since her return, but he had just glimpsed the old Freddie, and she wasn't happy. "That's it for now, Bessie. I'll give your nurse instructions to make sure you get your new meds and new diet."

"Diet? Now, you're trying to kill me. You're all ganging up on me."

Had he thought of Bessie as one of his most difficult patients? He elevated her to number one on his list. "I want you to eat more fruits and vegetables and cut out the fried foods."

Bessie pouted and sank into her covers. "Get out of here, boy, before you depress me more. I need a nap."

Gladly. "As you wish. I'm going to tell your nurse and your daughters, so you can't fool them."

"Killjoy." She clicked the remote control and turned Jerry Springer off, much to Trace's relief.

He escaped and went in search of the Applegate women. He nearly knocked Freddie down when he literally ran into her in the hall. Hostility vibrated off her, and he stepped back. "I didn't mean what you thought I meant back there."

"Now, you read minds, too? You're a multi-talented man. Should I ooh and ah?" She tried to sidestep him, but he blocked her path. He still needed to speak to her.

"You looked crestfallen when I said I didn't want to get married. It's nothing personal…"

"Look. I saw how you nearly swallowed your tongue when Mom inserted her foot in her mouth. Don't worry about me. I know Angel's more your type." She craned her neck to look up at him, her eyes flashing fire.

It was his turn to bristle. "Now, you're a mind reader? How would you know what my type is?"

She circled him like a vulture, ready to pick his mind clean. "You'd be surprised how much I know. Let's take inventory. You obviously put a lot of store in physical beauty or you wouldn't pump yourself up this way. And you crave luxury. You drive a Lexus. You remodeled your house. You like flashy women."

"What flashy women?" *Did she know about Skye Blue? She couldn't.* She was just talking out of her head, being stubborn and opinionated as usual.

She hesitated. Blush colored the apple of her cheeks. "My sister, for one."

"For two?" He held his breath. He preferred nobody knew about his thing for the singer or their clandestine night. *Could he have ended up on some tabloid cover with the superstar and not know it?* His reputation would be shot to hell if some camera-happy photographer snapped his picture going into Skye Blue's love den, and especially if they heard the ménage a trois part.

She finally said, "Theresa Coffey from high school. And Melody Blake, Stacey Kinnard, Chloe Oswald, and Hilary English — the entire cheerleading squad."

Oh, them. Well, they were fun and cute. What red-blooded American guy would deny himself their pleasures if offered? He'd been a football player and wrestler back then, so he'd had his pick of women. But that was high school and this was real life.

Except real life seemed more dreamlike of late...

"Can we just drop this now? You have anything else to tell me?" She was dismissing him, and he didn't like it. He was the doctor, and she was the patient. Most clients hung on his every word.

"I just want to go over your mother's new diet with you. Don't let her wiggle out of it. I've been on her back for years to eat better. Now, it has to be enforced." He scribbled down a quick list of good and bad foods, tore the paper from his binder, and held it out to her.

She perused it, and shook her head. "What? No peanut butter and banana sandwiches allowed? She's going to hate this."

Her sarcasm annoyed him but he tried to ignore it. The chip on her shoulder had snowballed into a boulder. "Just see that she sticks to her. I'll be back tomorrow to look in on her."

"Gotcha." She escorted him to the door and ushered him out as if she was eager to see his backside.

What was bothering her? He hadn't done or said anything offensive. He climbed into his car and headed for the gym to work out some of his frustration.

* * * * *

Wendy watched Trace leave, at war with herself. He electrified her, but he only had eyes for Skye Blue. *What would he say if he knew that dull, ugly Wendy Applegate transformed into the exotic Skye Blue? That he had fucked her?*

He'd probably run away screaming as fast as he could to delouse himself. She hauled her ugly ass to her mother's room, checked on the snoring beauty, and then wore a path to her bedroom. She flung herself on her bed and stared at her ceiling. She knew the ceiling well, down to the water spot that had never been painted over.

Who was she deluding? Trace looked at her as if she was a bug. He'd never looked at her adoringly, or with pure, unadulterated lust like he had gazed upon her alter ego. He'd never touch her like he'd touched Skye Blue.

Still, she couldn't forget the feel of his hot hands or even hotter lips. His tongue gave new meaning to the word 'erotic'. If all the tongues in the world were judged, his would win the blue ribbon. What it had done to…

Her nucleus throbbed, yearning for his touch. Familiar dampness spread between her legs and she moaned. Trace didn't deserve her love. Not even her lust. So, why couldn't she stop thinking about him? Why had she taken him to her couch and let him do such kinky things to her?

But her body wouldn't listen and demanded release. It must have smelled Trace's cock. It had behaved itself in L.A. when he was a country away, when she didn't run into him around every corner, and when he wasn't showing up at her concerts.

Thunder or Lightning would happily satisfy her carnal urges, but she didn't want to start something she couldn't handle, or rather something else she couldn't handle.

Flames licked her vagina that wouldn't stop. Slipping her hand inside her panties, she found her clit. Fingering the sensitive nub, it beaded at her touch, quivering. But, it wasn't enough.

If only Trace were here and loved her, not Skye Blue! She'd gladly trade her fame and fortune for his love. Locking her door, she pulled down her blinds, and turned on some smooth jazz to keep her in a romantic mood, then lit jasmine incense that she found in her drawer.

She moved a few boxes in the bottom of her closet, and ran her hand along the edge of the floorboards, looking for her secret hiding place where she'd stored her sex toys before she'd left home. Prying up the loose floorboard, she prayed her family hadn't found it. If they had, they'd left it in its spot, for the encased vibrator met her starved gaze. "Yes!"

Quivering in anticipation, she took fresh lubricating jelly from her suitcase, and oiled its smooth length. She divested the bed of the quilt, stripped her clothing, lay back on her bed, and spread her legs wide.

She closed her eyes and a jolt of pure yearning slammed through her at the memory of Trace in his sexy-as-hell leather breeches that had clearly delineated every bulge in his pants. Her flesh heating, she imagined that Trace circled her nipples with feather-light fingertips, and she moaned aloud. Then she squeezed the tightening buds, just as he had done. She caressed her breasts for several minutes until her greedy pussy demanded attention.

Her fingers skimmed over her flat abdomen, past her navel, and sought her clitoris. Writhing, her control long since in tatters, she rubbed her hot spot. Lifting her hips off the bed, she gyrated in slow motion.

Letting it slide along her highly sensitized folds, the big cock teased her vagina. Self-torture and deprivation weren't her style, so she stretched her lips and inserted the tip of the rod. The vibrator was almost as thick and long as Trace's cock, and she plunged it deep inside her. She squeezed it with her vaginal muscles as she thrust it in and out.

Her blood humming fast and furious through her veins, a light sweat breaking out on her brow, moans escaped her lips. Wave after wave of pleasure wracked her, and she bit back a scream. Ravenous, she slammed the cock in harder, as fast as her hips could meet the frantic thrusts.

She could still see Trace's cock pounding in and out, could still feel his fire setting her ablaze. His passion carried her away, and soon, the bed rocked beneath her.

Desperate hunger for Trace consuming her, she squeezed the cock as tightly as she could. Liquid fire pooled in her womb and orgasms shuddered through her. Her long hair a damp tangle around her, she trembled, spent. Smiling dreamily, she snuggled up to her oversized pillow, wishing the real man would hold her.

Chapter Five

The phone shrilled, waking Wendy from an erotic dream in which Trace drank of her lips, and knew the true identity of the woman he kissed and caressed. Not wishing to awaken, she groaned.

By the time she found the phone in her jeans pocket, the ringing had stopped, so she checked her messages. Thunder's cell phone number read out on the digital display. The time caught her eye and she gasped. *Four hours late for rehearsal! The band was going to kill her.*

She wrapped a sheet around her, toga style, and then hit redial. "I'm so sorry. I fell asleep and didn't know what time it was."

"You weren't answering your phone, either. You sleeping with that fan from the other night?" Irritation flowed through Thunder's voice. *Or was that jealousy?* She hoped not.

His irritation infected her and she scrunched up her nose as she paced the floor. "In my mother's house? Are you nuts?"

He ignored her and rushed into another thought. "You know we have another gig Friday in Tallahassee and we don't have the new song down yet. Think you can haul your sweet buns over here now? I don't want to see you forget the words onstage."

"Let me shower, and I'll be there in a jiff." She grimaced at the hateful watch that told her it was ten P.M.

She hoped she hadn't missed a call from her mother while she slept. "I have to check on Mom, too."

"Don't stand us up again, or I'll be forced to come get you."

Thunder, here? In her home? The threat catapulted her into action. She didn't trust him not to say or do something outrageous to get her into trouble. "*No!* Don't do that. I'm on my way."

Wendy snapped the phone shut, and ducked into the shower to sluice the musky scent from her flesh. Then she dressed in her favorite all-black clothing and tied her hair into a high ponytail, feeling like a sixteen-year-old commando on a secret mission.

As she walked across the threshold into the muggy Florida night, Angel flitted into the room. "Well, well. Another clandestine midnight rendezvous?"

Wendy tried to keep her mask on but felt it slipping. "If you mean, am I sneaking out to meet a lover? No. I'm meeting friends."

"At this hour?" Angel tsk-tsked.

She was an independent twenty-eight year old, and the nurse was safely tucked in the room next to her mother, so she had nothing to be apologetic about. "Yep. I've got my cell phone. Call if there's an emergency."

Then she remembered that the last time she'd said that, her sister had suffered a terrible emergency and called her home. Her flat iron had gone on the fritz and she couldn't straighten her hair. "A real emergency only. Such as if Mom's condition gets much worse."

"It's an emergency every time I call you. But it's really rotten that you don't want to talk to me. Or that you never invite me to hang out with your friends. All of a sudden you're Miss Popularity."

Wendy's jaw almost hit the floor. Angel had never wanted to hang out with her before. And Angel had been the one in the popular crowd. She hadn't wanted Wendy horning in on her group of friends. There wasn't time to get into a free-for-all right now. Thunder might make good on his threat. "I'm afraid I can't ask you to join us this time, but we'll do something together soon. Tomorrow. Maybe we can split a pizza at Antonio's."

Disbelief glittered in Angel's eyes. "Pizza? I can't eat pizza. If you were here more, paid more attention, you'd know I was on a strict diet. Every roll shows up in the swimsuit competition and that's all it takes to get kicked out of the finals."

Suddenly, Wendy felt obese in her size six denims compared to her sister's svelte size two. "Salad, then. Do they still have that fab salad bar?"

Angel stuck out her lower lip. "I can't tomorrow. I have rehearsal for my talent and another fitting of my gowns. I could use some support."

Wendy had a lot of rehearsing to do herself if she wanted to be ready in time for Friday. "What's your talent?"

"Singing. You're not the only songbird in the family, you know." Angel preened and cleared her throat. Without any further encouragement from Wendy, she massacred a Top Ten pop tune.

Wendy tried not to wince, but the off-key pitch grated down her spine. Angel's pronunciation and breathing were all off, too. She prayed her sister had time to work on her talent. "When is the next pageant?"

"You forgot?" Her sister's countenance didn't merely look crestfallen, but destroyed. "How could you forget? It's Saturday up in Ocala. You're going up with me Friday…"

Friday! Wendy gasped. "I can't possibly go with you Friday. I'm sorry, Angel."

"You promised! I can't do this on my own."

"Do you have a friend that could go with you?" Wendy backed out the door, extremely conscious that time was slipping away, and with it, her career.

"I want my sister." Pain flashed in Angel's eyes so quickly that Wendy wondered if her imagination was playing tricks on her.

The sentiment was so sweet, Wendy's heart twisted. She hugged her sister close. "Maybe I can join you Saturday morning. Will that be in time?" Of course she'd be wiped out from the grueling night before, but she had to make the effort. *Isn't that why God invented caffeine?*

"What's so very important that you can't cancel?" Angel twirled her diamond ear stud.

"My job."

"On a Friday night?" Disbelief rang in her sister's voice.

"Yes. We have a big client presentation which will go late." Wendy's head started to pound with the tick tock of the clock and her sister's endless questions.

Her cell phone shrilled again and she turned it off, knowing Thunder must be trying to track her down. "That must be them paging me now. Gotta go. Don't wait up for me."

"I won't," Angel said dryly, standing by the door.

Wendy skipped down the front steps, the motion sensor illuminating the garden path to the driveway. A convention of geckos and baby frogs smaller than her index finger scampered up the side of the house and undercover of her mother's azalea bushes.

Unfortunately, she didn't frighten the mosquito that buzzed in her face. All she needed was to contract Yellow Fever or West Nile Virus. She batted her attacker away and sprinted to her car before the rest of his bloodsucking friends swarmed her.

She turned on the CD of the new song that Lightning had copied for her and sang along, warming up her voice. The streets had been rolled back and most of the living room lights of the houses in town had been dimmed. Only starlight and her headlights lit the road, leaving her to squint in the darkness.

Halfway to the rental house, she noticed the car behind her had been following her for a while. It hung back, but kept pace with her, slowing when she slowed and speeding up when she sped up. She swore under her breath. The glare of its headlights blinded her so that she couldn't make out the make or model of the vehicle. However, she bet it was her sister.

She considered calling home to see if Angel answered the phone, but thought better of it as the ringing might wake her mother. Instead, she called Thunder. "Hey, Dude. I ran into a little snag and I'm running late. I'll be there as soon as I can."

"What little snag? We've rescheduled our lives and dragged our butts across the country to accommodate you, so maybe you shouldn't blow us off like this." Guitars warmed up in the background.

She negotiated a sharp bend with one hand and cursed the phone when she realized how close to the canal the car's tire had skidded. She'd forgotten that out in the country, some of the canals hugged the two lane roads, and the remembered knowledge unnerved her. She'd have to get a hands-free kit for talking in the car.

She gritted her teeth. "I appreciate your sacrifices. I do. And I'm not blowing you off. My sister wouldn't let me out of the house and now she's following me. I have to lose her before I can come to the house."

"Maybe you should just come clean and bring her along. The rest of our families know about us."

She snarled, thinking of Angel's reaction. "The rest of your families aren't news hungry. Angelina might leak our secret to the press to enhance her chances of becoming the next Miss America."

"Would it be so terrible if everyone knew our true identities? Other bands survive."

She glanced at the eerie headlights in her rear view mirror and shuddered. What if the car following her wasn't Angel's? What if it was some other creep? "And be hounded and followed the rest of our lives? Believe me, you should get a taste of this to see how much you like it."

"Maybe you should give her a little more credit," he said on a long-suffering sigh. "But I can't make up your mind. Try to shake her and get here before dawn breaks. Rain's inhaling all the caffeine pills to prop her eyes open."

Nothing like a little guilt with his lecture. "Maybe we should reschedule for tomorrow morning when we're all fresh and wide awake?"

"How about I come and get you tomorrow morning so you won't dodge us again? I won't let little sis boss you around." Soft strumming underlined his words.

She had no doubt he would carry through his threat. "No."

"You ashamed of us? Don't you want your urban family to meet your mom and little sister?" He paused, and asked sharply, "That car still following you? Maybe you should hang up with me and call the cops. Or better yet, stay on with me and I'll have Lightning call them on his cell."

She checked behind her again and saw a very dim set of lights illuminating the windy road. "Someone's there, but I can't tell if it's the same car." Spooked now, she pulled over at the first open convenience store she found and took her cell phone inside, then waited by the window for the car to pass.

After a good fifteen minutes had passed and there was no sign of the other car, she called Thunder back. "Come and get me. He's still not passed by. I don't know if he turned off the road or if he's waiting for me to pull out. I don't like this at all."

"Nor do I, luv. I knew I shouldn't have let you leave civilization for this swamp. Now, give me directions and we'll bring you back here."

* * * * *

Wendy fell asleep on the couch after only a few sets. Waking up slowly, she rubbed the sleep from her eyes. Her back cramped and sore, she missed her soft feather bed back home.

"Rise and shine, sleepy head. Let's get some groceries into you and then practice the set again. There are still a few rough spots to iron out."

Bright sunlight pierced her eyes, making her squint. Adrenalin pumped through her veins and she jumped to her feet. "What time is it?" Her mother probably had the cops out looking for her. And they would find her deserted car at the gas station. *Oh, yeah, she was really following doctor's advice.*

"Quarter past noon. We didn't finish up till three in the morning so we all slept in." Thunder yawned through his words, obviously just waking up himself as well.

She raked her fingers through her mussed hair, then slung her purse over her shoulder. "I have to go home now. Will you take me?"

"But what about practice? We were going to have some lunch and then start over." A dark frown marred his masculine beauty.

"Fine. I'll call a cab." She dragged her cell phone out of her pocket.

Before she could flip it open, Thunder sighed and curled his fingers around it, preventing her from opening it. "If you insist. Hop in my chariot. Just let me tell the others."

"Tell them I'm very sorry. I'll visit with my mother, make sure she's okay, then I'll come back. Promise." She restrained the absurd desire to cross her heart.

Thunder folded his burly arms over his chest. "I've heard that one before."

Torn in two, feeling guilty as hell no matter what she did, she rubbed her forehead. "Give me a break. I'm doing the best I can. I'd understand if it was your family."

Her friend's expression softened and he lowered his arms. "I know you would. But this business is dog-eat-dog at the best of times. The competition doesn't care how it gets one up on us. If they sense a weak spot, they'll drag us down."

"Maybe it's time to retire." Then she could devote her time to her family and just be herself again. *Her nobody, invisible self?*

"You crazy? Just because it's tough doesn't mean we should lie down and die." He dug his keys out of his pants pocket, jangled them, and helped her into his car.

Although the mosquitoes didn't venture out in daylight hours, he wound up the windows and cranked on the air conditioning. The hot Florida sun had baked the car and steam rolled out the doors. The black leather seats, which looked so pretty, burned her arms. A branding iron couldn't sizzle hotter than the seat belts.

She pulled her shades out of her purse and slid them onto the bridge of her nose. All this nightlife had turned her into a vampire. Sunlight hurt her eyes and she couldn't fathom venturing outside without her UV-filtered lenses.

Thunder whistled under his breath when they arrived at the store and pulled up next to her car. "Someone had fun vandalizing your wheels."

Chills skipped down her spine. The tires were AWOL. All of the windows were smashed. Dents scarred the hood and shards of glass littered the ground beneath the busted headlights. "Do you think it was just a bunch of naughty kids? Or that whoever was following me did this?"

"I don't know. Either way, they did a load of damage. Perhaps we should take you back to L.A. and get you out of here. Better safe than sorry."

"Mom's going to flip out. They totaled it." Her mother freaked out over small cuts. Trace didn't want her mother upset in her current condition and she would find this very disturbing.

Then her coworker's words sank in. "I can't leave Mom yet. She's still sick. And Roger rescheduled all our concerts around here anyway."

"I'll take you home but we're not done discussing this." Promise rang in Thunder's words.

"It was probably just kids with too much time on their hands." She repeated it more to convince herself than her friend. Kids wouldn't mean her any personal harm. She had nothing to worry about.

"Maybe." He slid a serious glance at her. "Maybe not. The police have to be informed."

"I don't want them worrying my mother when she's sick! They'll need to look at the car anyway, so let's call them here and hopefully they won't show up on my doorstep."

What seemed like several hours later, Thunder pulled into her driveway. Sweaty, stressed out, and starved, she couldn't handle one more problem today, so she groaned when she spied Trace's Lexus parked by her sister's car.

"Thanks for the lift. Just drop me here."

"You sure I can't come in and meet your mother? She doesn't have to know my stage name."

Her heart beat frantically, hoping Trace didn't choose this moment to wander outside. She slipped from the car and closed the door as silently as she could so the sound wouldn't carry inside to notify the occupants of the house that she was home. "I promise I'll introduce you soon as she's feeling up to visitors."

He sighed deeply and drummed his fingers on the dashboard. "I'll pick you up at seven tonight. Be ready to sing your heart out."

Her friend's brow lifted and a devilish smile played on his lips. He tilted his head at the house. "I've seen that guy somewhere before. Isn't he that chap that you were..."

Chapter Six

She didn't look behind her. Of course it had to be Trace. She had the worst luck in the world. She couldn't remember if Thunder had still worn his grease paint the night he interrupted their lovemaking, or not. She wasn't going to chance recognition or something totally embarrassing and incriminating coming out of her friend's mouth.

"Of course not. I never met that man before. The sun must be in your eyes." She waved it off as nothing, hoping he would lose interest.

"I got a pretty good look at the dude and they could be twins." Thunder leaned over her, gaping out the window, embarrassing her. Worse, she had been naked in all her glory and he'd gotten a good look at Trace? She was highly insulted. He should've been mesmerized by her great bod.

"Where were you all night, Missy? And where's your car?" Wendy's mother hobbled onto the porch and greeted her with a hostile stare.

She glared at Thunder until he retreated to his side of the car and treated Trace to a similarly recriminating glare, but the power play didn't pan out when she had to look way up at him. "Why did you let her out of bed?"

Brimstone boiled in Trace's normally cool eyes. "Let her? I'm not the one who stayed out all night without calling. Nor am I the one who wrecked the car."

Wendy's mouth went dry and she gulped. "How'd she find out about the car?"

Bessie leaned heavily on her cane as if she was ninety instead of fifty-one. She swayed and then plopped onto the wooden porch swing. "When we called the police to file a missing person's report, they filled us in."

Unbelievable! Yes, she should have called, so it was primarily her fault. But it hadn't been twenty-four hours yet and she was a self-supporting twenty-eight year old. *Did Mick Jagger and Madonna get treated like a child when they went home?*

She checked her attitude. If the situation was reversed, she'd have been worried, too. "It was a rental car…"

Bessie harrumphed and lifted her nose high. "Insurance doesn't cover everything. Sales clerks don't make enough to fix totaled cars. Don't be asking me for a loan to help you out. I hope you won't have to work three jobs to pay it off."

Not with the put downs again. Ugh! Wendy ground her teeth. How she wanted to scream, but she contained herself with great restraint. "You worry too much about money. Why didn't you just call me? I told Angel I had my cell phone."

"We did, but you didn't pick up. You worried twenty-five years off my life thinking you lay dead in some canal." Her mother smoothed her wrinkled nightdress over her knees, her hands trembling.

Wendy dragged her cellular out of her purse and checked it. *Great.* "The battery's dead." She seemed to be murdering everything of a mechanical or electronic nature. She was a virtual Bermuda's Triangle.

She hugged her mother and kissed her on the cheek. "I'm really sorry. I didn't know the phone was dead or that I had overslept. I wouldn't intentionally worry you."

Bessie kissed her starchly, and then pulled back, a speculative gleam in her eyes. "Just whose bed did you oversleep in? Mr. Hair's?"

Wendy swallowed a gasp. "I'm an adult. It's my business with whom and where I sleep."

Then when she noticed Trace sneaking sideways glances at her, she added, "I fell asleep on the couch. I have the kink in my neck to prove it." She twisted around and tried to massage the killer cramp to no avail. Her maneuvering made it worse and a moan escaped her lips.

Empathy welled with anger in the doctor's gaze. Finally, he strode over to her, his expression dark. "Stand up and turn around."

"Why?" Suspicion wrapped around her heart as she complied with his directions. "Are you a chiropractor now, too?"

"Do you want to feel better or wallow in your misery?" All commiseration had drained from his voice and his eyes held about as much compassion as a raven's. Rather, he sounded as if he'd rather strangle her. That begged the question why? He had the hots for Skye Blue, not Freddie Applegate.

"Me wallow?" A-type personalities didn't wallow. They took action. She had to be fit for the Tallahassee gig the next evening. "Never. Fix it, Mister Miracle Worker."

"That's Doctor Miracle Worker to you." Before she realized his intention, he hauled her against his strong chest, lifted her off her feet, and cracked her back.

Blinding hot pain seared across her spine. Yelps of pain tore from her lips. And then blessed relief stole over her, all in the space of a moment. As she gulped in air, Trace's arms loosened around her ribs. His chest felt too warm, too vibrant against her back, and she shivered. Her traitorous body wanted to mold itself to his. He was too hot to be legal.

But she was trapped. Red alert sirens blared in her head. Only Skye Blue could take such liberties and get away with them—Skye Blue who hid her ordinary features beneath glittery makeup and a diva's attitude. Furious at her self-made plight, she wrenched away from him and mumbled, "Thanks. You know your stuff. I owe you."

That only brought vivid memories to mind of just how well he knew his other stuff—how to please a woman. How to drive her insane with longing and ecstasy. *But how could she repay him as Wendy? She couldn't.*

Since she couldn't turn around and hold him like she wanted, she needed her sex toy soon as she could escape. She backed away toward the open door. "You okay now, Mom? How about I fix you something to eat and then I'll go clean up?"

Her mother nodded, rose to her feet and ambled to her room. "I need a nap after all this excitement. This old heart can't take such upset. I lost my appetite. I'm going to bed."

Wendy tucked her mother into her bed and made sure she lay comfortably and had cool water and a clean tumbler within reaching distances. Still, twinges of guilt attacked her. She looked to Trace to make sure it was okay if her mother skipped lunch.

He nodded. "I have other patients to see. I'll check in on her before I leave tomorrow."

Adrenalin gushed through her veins. *Leave? Tomorrow?* Where was he going for the weekend? To Angel's pageant? Or to see Skye Blue again? She ordered her wild heart to be still lest he hear her excitement. Casually as she could muster, she asked, "You going away for the weekend?"

"Doctors have personal lives, too." A secret smile hovered around his chiseled lips, and strategic shadows hid the expression in his eyes. He didn't volunteer more than that to her chagrin.

He'd be surprised how much she understood about his personal life. It was all she could do to keep a straight face. Immediate escape was imperative before he discovered her secret, even if that meant she couldn't trick any more information out of him.

Great! Now, she'd be distracted the entire concert seeking a glimpse of her leather-clad lover. Perhaps she should lip sync to her own songs to make sure she didn't screw them up.

"I'm going to get cleaned up and take a nap. If you'll excuse me..." She didn't wait for an answer, just pivoted on her worn heel and made her getaway.

Wendy made a beeline to her secret hiding place, took her vibrator out of its box, and installed new batteries. Then she remembered the door wasn't locked so she crossed the floor to secure her privacy.

But Angel barged in, battle sparkling in her eyes, a moment before she reached it. "Now, see what you've done? I told you not to duck out at midnight. Mama's been in a frenzy all day. I had to call Trace over to give her something to calm her down."

Wendy's heart stopped and she tried to hide the sex toy behind her back as unobtrusively as possible, if it was possible to hide a ten-inch dildo without being noticed. "Uh, have you ever heard of knocking and waiting to be invited into someone's bedroom?" Heat suffused her cheeks and her breathing grew shallow.

"What are you hiding?" Angel tackled her, reaching around her and grabbing for Wendy's vibrator.

Determined, Wendy wasn't about to let her sister see her secret. Unfortunately, Angel was equally determined and they scuffled for possession.

"It's mine." Wendy gritted her teeth so hard her gums ached. Her sister was no powder puff and fought like a wildcat.

Angel's sharp nails clawed her, making Wendy wince. Redoubling her efforts, she jerked away and crashed into her dresser, knocking several perfume bottles to the floor in ear-splintering chaos.

Her sister yanked the vibrator away, held it up, and stared at it cross-eyed, shuddering. "Ewww."

Footsteps pounded down the hallway, and the women froze, staring at each other.

Not good!

"What's going on in here? You okay?" Trace's shadow fell into the room ominously, and then he filled the doorway. His brow furrowed.

Panicked, mortified, Wendy uttered a whispered plea. "Please don't tell them. I'll owe you big time." She held her breath, imploring her sister to be her ally.

White as a ghost, Angel thrust the toy at her. "Lock your door from now on. I know nothing," she said in her best Sergeant Schultz' imitation.

Wendy breathed a sigh of relief and smiled at her sister as she took it back and tried to hide it surreptitiously. "Will do."

"Will do what, Missy?" Bessie's sharp tones startled her so much, she dropped the incriminating evidence.

All blood drained from Wendy's face and her sockets opened too wide for her eyes. She swallowed hard. *Where was a killer-earth-swallowing-quake when she needed one?*

"It's not mine," Wendy and Angel said in unison. Their harmony sounded patently false to her own ears. They looked like a pair of guilty poltergeists.

"Leave us alone, Angelina. Close the door behind you." Bessie bore down on Wendy as Angel scurried from the room as if reprieved from a firing squad. Then, as if she had eyes in the back of her head, her mother said, "Stay, Trace."

Wendy squared her shoulders and reminded herself that she was twenty-eight and an independent, sexually free woman. Then she kicked the apparatus under her bed and swore to throw it into the deepest canal she could find.

Bessie crawled under the bed and retrieved it to Wendy's absolute horror. She held it up, turned it around, and examined the intricate detail. Waving it under Trace's nose, Bessie asked, "Tell me, Doctor. Is it normal for a thirty-two-year-old woman to use one of these?"

Wendy squirmed, bit back a moan, and snuck glances at Trace through her lowered lashes. Ultimate disgrace. Lifetime blackmail material. She'd never live this down.

This was far worse than when Thunder had solicited them for a threesome.

Trace gaped at the damn thing, then stared at her. His Adam's apple worked hard and the pulse in his neck beat erratically. "No. I mean yes, many normal women use them."

Bessie shook it in the air, making the rubber shaft warble. "I mean, is it normal for a thirty-two-year-old woman not to have a man of her own?"

Wendy counted to ten and groaned. "I'm only twenty-eight. Just a few moments ago, you accused me of sleeping with Thun—Ian." She bit her tongue. *What a deadly mistake she'd almost made. Cripes!* "You can't have it both ways. Do you want me to be sexually repressed, or don't you?"

Bessie's jaw dropped and she gaped at Wendy. Finally she said, "I can't believe my ears. I knew L.A. was the devil's den. Trace, tell her she needs a real man in her bed, like you."

Stunned silence suffocated her as she locked gazes with the object of all her sexual fantasies. His shallow breaths taunted her. *What was he thinking? Surely not what she was. He probably wished aliens would abduct him.*

Snapping to her senses, Wendy rescued him from a fate worse than death. "Thank you, Mama Matchmaker, but we're both mature adults capable of choosing our own mates."

She plucked the so-dead-and-gone vibrator from her mother's paws. "I'll just go hack this into tiny pieces and burn it now." Even if she ever used another sex toy in her long life, it wouldn't be one her family had handled. *In her sister's very articulate words, eewww!*

Trace grimaced and squirmed. Too late, she remembered to be sensitive to his man's worst nightmare. *Oh, well. He'll live.* She only had it out for the rubber snake.

"I still think she needs to see a psychiatrist. She has no direction in her life. She'll wind up sixty, broke, and alone except for that thing."

Aggravated to the extreme, Wendy sighed and rubbed her throbbing temples. When she looked up, she expected to see pity or disgust, perhaps even sympathy in Trace's eyes. Instead, he rocked her world when his gaze bore into her with raw sexual prowess.

Her heart flipped over in her chest. *What was she in for now?* Trace would tease her till the day she died. She supposed teasing rated above disgust or pity, but would be far worse in the long run. How long could she hide her secret if he decided to torment her? He threatened her sanity now.

"I'm not broke or alone," she said in a singsong voice. "I'm very happy with my life." She was far ahead of the ten-year plan she'd devised in college, far beyond her wildest dreams, save one thing… Her gaze drifted to the amused doctor again.

Bessie clapped her hands. "Prove it. Bring Mr. Hair to dinner."

"I'm sure he'd love to, but…he was just on his way to the airport. He'll be out of town for a long time…indefinitely." She was getting too adept at lying. *She was going to burn in hell.*

"Soon as he gets back, you bring that young man over here to meet me." Bessie yawned.

Wendy flopped on her bed, gazed at her paint-flaked ceiling and wrinkled her nose. Cheap perfume permeated the air, choking her.

Trace cleared his throat, reminding her that they were alone. Something flickered in his eyes, but disappeared too quickly for her to interpret.

"Stop gloating." If she had a spiky shoe handy, she'd throw it at him. Luckily for him, no projectiles lay within grabbing distance.

"Who's gloating?" Sinfully sexy and husky, his deep voice tried to seduce her.

Who was she kidding? She was no beauty queen, no sexy Skye Blue. Skye Blue was a lovely fantasy that paid her rent.

"Laughing, then." She glared at his handsome face, his movie star-teeth, his dreamy eyes, his Grecian nose. Pretty boy probably had so many women lined up, he'd never need a sex toy. He didn't need her scalp in his collection. "Leave me alone in my misery. Let me die quietly of embarrassment." When he didn't move a muscle to leave, she added, "Don't you have patients waiting?"

The mattress depressed as he sat beside her on the bed, an expression dangerously near sympathy welling in his eyes. "Will you be all right?"

She rolled toward him and leaned on her elbow. "So now, you agree with Mom? Are you a psychiatrist, too?" He could be the most renowned shrink in the world and she'd never reveal the depth of her soul to him.

He captured her hand and squeezed it gently, then rubbed the pad of his thumb over her knuckles, surprising her. "I'm not the enemy, Freddie. I want us to be friends again."

Only friends? Had they ever been friends? Could she take just being friends with him?

Electric current zapped her hand. It took everything she possessed not to squirm or ravage him. Her lips ached to caress the hand holding hers.

When shudders racked her down to her core, she yanked her hand away lest he detect them and understood their source. "If you're my friend, you'd call me Wendy. Freddie sounds like a decrepit old man with a wooden peg leg and a glass eye."

Trace chuckled, his buttery voice tickling her ears. He leaned over her, pinning her to the bed, and stole her breath. "You have no imagination whatsoever, do you, Wendy?"

His breath teased her lips, crept into her mouth, intoxicating her. No one had ever uttered her name so erotically or seductively. She was in danger of melting in his arms, of forgetting who she was, and in particular, where she was.

Those lips hypnotized her, so close, so firm, yet so soft. If she were to kiss him, would he recognize her taste? How could he not instinctively know her? Her hormones had a lock on him. She'd know his scent, his touch, anywhere, in any disguise. And a physician should be more discerning than a rock star.

Parched, starved, but not for food or water, she licked her lips. She struggled to keep her head. Trace wasn't attracted to her. He was playing with her. His blood ran hot for Skye Blue and the glamorous people. "And you don't have a sense of humor, do you?"

"What's that supposed to mean?" Trace's gaze crystallized on her. His features turned to stone and his muscles tensed.

Resolving to save face, she pushed him off her and rolled off the other side of her bed. Stretching to her full, unimpressive height, she faced off against him, her courage returning with the queen-sized bed separating them. "Don't make fun of me, Trace. I didn't like it as a kid and I don't like it now."

"I never…"

She held up her hand to stop his lies. "Don't lie. I overheard you tell my sister you thought her much prettier and much more to your liking than me." The old pain bore down on her, making it difficult to breathe.

Trace froze. He paled. "God, Freddie. I didn't mean for you to hear that. I was a kid. I didn't mean it."

She shielded her heart and lifted her chin. "Kids usually say exactly what they mean. They're more brutally honest than adults who play games."

"You think I'm playing a game?"

"I don't know what you're doing but I don't like it." First he seduced Skye Blue. Now, he flirted with her? Should Skye Blue be jealous like she was?

Bring on the shrink. She was certifiably schizophrenic and didn't know who she was anymore.

"I'm not sure what was happening, either, but do you have to dissect and analyze everything? Can't you just let things happen naturally?" Anger and confusion brewed in his voice. He raked unsteady fingers through his hair, making him look more like her leather lover.

She sucked in her breath. "Don't even pretend you're interested in me. Your eyes glazed over the moment you saw my, my…"

"Big cock?"

She gasped, unprepared to hear the all-American-boy-next-door-turned-doctor use such language. Of course, he might suffer from a dual personality same as she.

"Don't pretend to go prudish on me. I know better."

How dare he? Anger burst in her veins. She jerked a trembling finger at the door. "Get out."

* * * * *

What a little spitfire! As much or more than Skye Blue.

Freddie was a surprising, fascinating woman, much more than he'd ever dreamed. She was also the most exasperating wench in history, more trouble than she was worth.

Whatever had possessed him to come on to her? He'd been shocked to see her as a sexual creature, even more shocked when electricity had vibrated through them just holding her hand.

He'd wanted to kiss her, had been going to drink of her lips, when she'd turned into Psycho Woman and practically shoved him off her bed.

She was a case. Maybe her mother had been right in thinking Wendy needed counseling for that mountain on her shoulder. *No wonder her neck hurt.*

Malpractice insurance was burying him alive already. He couldn't afford extra life insurance against Freddie's attacks also. He'd steer clear.

He turned his mind to happier thoughts—this weekend's Storm concert in Tallahassee.

His cock sprung to life. He'd worried about it after Freddie had so graphically described mutilating the other one. *Ouch!* The thought was sufficient to make him lose his arousal. Just as well, he didn't want the lunatic to think he was hot for her. Or her mother to get more cockamamie ideas. Maybe it was time to turn this patient over to his partner. *Too bad he'd still live next-door to the psycho ward.*

He finished his rounds and then escaped to the gym to work off his tension. Unfortunately, Mr. Hair dominated the scene, a harem of lovely women swarming around him.

Recognition lit the other man's eyes when his gaze fell on Trace…and challenge?

Were they in competition over something? For Freddie?

A growl rose in Trace's chest. He didn't like it. That moron wasn't good enough for Freddie.

He didn't dare explore his feelings any deeper. But he showed that turkey who was stronger and bench-pressed fifty pounds more weight.

Chapter Seven

"Your boyfriend's here again." Thunder sidled up to Wendy onstage and whispered in her ear. He pointed out the leather-clad Viking in the front row. "I saw him at the gym yesterday. I know it was the same dude that was here."

Wendy's heart skipped several beats, and she struggled to stay nonchalant. She forced herself not to seek Trace out yet and get spun up in Thunder's hallucinations, but her respiration shallowed and she was jumpy.

"That's nice." *Why was Thunder so weirded out by this?* He had relinquished all claims on her when he married Carly.

"Who is he?"

Wendy waved to her adoring crowd, smiling brilliantly under the interrogation. "Just a fan."

"My ass. You wouldn't even kiss me till the fourth date. And that is the fellow that was strutting around your house like he owned it. Plus, he was mighty cozy with your mother, the mother you won't introduce me to." Rage flashed in Thunder's eyes. *And jealousy?*

Lord save her. She swallowed her apprehension. "That guy? He's just the boy-next-door and now, he's Mom's doctor. Up close, he doesn't look a thing like that Orlando fan, if that is him. I'm amazed you can see anything under these killer lights."

"And I'm Diana Ross. Get your eyes checked, luv." Thunder tossed his unruly mane like the wild stallion he was, then thankfully, he moved away so she could breathe.

Trace's gaze dueled with hers, the passion in his intoxicating her.

Thunder returned, snorting. His nostrils flared.

Not another snit. She bit back a groan and almost choked on it.

"If you mean nothing to him and he means nothing to you, why was doctor-boy glaring at me at the gym yesterday?"

Her smile slipped and she gulped. It was a good thing she was sitting down on her piano bench for her knees went weak. *Why would Trace glare at Thunder?* The possibilities boggled her mind. "He was?"

"Ah hah! You admit it. You do know him. So, why all the cloak and dagger? Why doesn't he travel with you? Where did he get a backstage pass?"

She averted her gaze and made a concentrated effort not to bite her lip or do something equally gauche. Thankfully, Rain started the set with a crash of her cymbals, pulling Thunder back to his job.

Blessed reprieve. She owed a debt to Rain.

Thunder's glare told her she hadn't heard the end of this.

"You're delusional!" she mouthed with her back to the audience. "Did you forget your Prozac?" To her horror, the mike broadcast her slur through the coliseum despite her hand covering it. Had a room of 40,000 fans ever shut up so fast? The deathly quiet freaked her out.

His eyes feral, Thunder turned his back on the stunned crowd and growled at her.

She tried to redeem herself. "We can really act," she repeated into the mike. Then she mouthed, "I'm sorry."

He glowered at her and mouthed back, "I'll get you for this!"

She was so dead meat!

Trace's adoring gaze helped to chase away her demons. His sweat-slickened flesh glowed silver under the black lights. *Hubba hubba...luscious.*

She licked her lips, wishing she were licking him all over and then tossed him a come-hither smile. He would be salty and musky, just the way she remembered him. His taste lingered in her mouth, its memory fueling erotic fantasies. Pure testosterone would mask his usual hospital ammonia scent.

Trace's gaze devoured her. His lips curled into a drop-dead gorgeous smile, filling her with such ecstasy, she caressed the high notes longer than ever before.

She sang only to him, pouring her heart and soul into her song. The tones were more lush and sultrier than her favorite rendition of 'Carmen'.

Her lust transmitted itself to her fans. Couples made out. Grandmothers wept. Men tossed roses onstage so that red and yellow petals floated around her feet.

If only Trace would give her roses. She closed her eyes, her heart swelling with love, and pretended that Trace loved her, Wendy, with all her flaws and foibles.

Anguish colored her voice. Her lifelong dream stood so close...yet so far. Skye Blue could have Trace. Wendy never could. After her mother's interference, he must think her a pathetic old maid.

Singing the duet with Thunder later in the set had never been so trying. He bristled. He moved stiffly. No joy flowed in his voice. Howling cats sounded more musical than his clipped, angry words.

* * * * *

The dazzling songstress stole Trace's breath. Captivated, his eyes adored the sexiest creature on the planet.

Her steamy emerald eyes intoxicated him. Desire slammed through him and he would rather die than break eye contact. Their gazes dueled, and she sang to him.

Fire burned in his blood. His body throbbed. Magical, mysterious, she embodied the essence of his dreams. Like a randy teen, he drooled over America's darling, longing to crush her lips beneath his, to carry her away to his own private cave, and claim her as his.

She was the worst woman in the world for him. Wild rock stars didn't fit the notion of the ideal doctor's wife.

Crazy! His last brain cell had gone south and he was thinking with the wrong head. Why would America's darling give up her glamorous life for some nobody small-town doctor? Why should she choose just one man? Mr. Hair seemed to think she'd welcome a threesome.

How could he assuage her voracious appetite?

He planned to try tonight. His burgeoning arousal chafed painfully inside the tight leather pants. Last time should have taught him to wear something loose and baggy. But only a wild man would impress a wild woman. If he came on to her as a buttoned-down yuppie, she'd look straight through him.

* * * * *

About a century later, the final notes of the concert faded. Good thing as Wendy's nerves couldn't take any more. *She was so out of here.*

She fled Thunder's wrath, hopefully into Trace's arms. Purple stars danced in front of her eyes as if she'd been staring into the sun. Those lights were brutal.

"Remember me?" Trace's beloved, husky voice whispered in her ear. His warm breath seared her ear, making her shiver.

Mischievous fairies frolicked in her chest and she whirled around, her hair billowing about her. She started to purr, "Of course," then choked back her words. Since she couldn't speak to him aloud, she stood on tiptoe and pressed her lips to his. When her breasts grazed his warm chest, tingles raked her.

His eyes blazed down into hers, igniting a forest fire between her legs. Consumed by the fire, she linked her fingers through his and pulled him behind her. "Your throat still sore?" Trace asked when she remained silent.

She tossed her best Mona Lisa smile his way, and she shook her head slowly. He could draw his own conclusions.

When they neared her room, Thunder separated himself from the shadows. He'd been waiting for her. Storm clouds chased across his face.

Not Hurricane Thunder again!

"Red alert," Trace whispered in her ear. His fingers tightened around hers. "Am I usurping his claim?"

Her heart skipped several beats. *Never!* She shook her head violently and pointed to her door then Trace's chest. The testosterone rose to explosive levels. Hurricane

Thunder was ready to strike, and judging by the way Trace bristled, he was, too.

"You want to go to my room?"

She nodded vigorously, imploring him with her eyes to go. Later, privately, she'd deal with Thunder and his bizarre behavior. At least he was in makeup, so Trace wouldn't recognize him as Mr. Hair. She prayed not, anyway.

Camera flashes blinded her when they tried to sneak out the back of the coliseum. The crush of fans suffocated her and her blood pressure jumped. She pulled Trace around to try and hide his face from the cameras.

"The life of the rich and famous?" Trace grumbled barely loud enough for her to hear under the din.

She grimaced. Not the best part of her day. Where was her genie to pouf them out of here? Where was her fairy godmother?

Never, never again would she practice such lunacy as to venture outside as her alter ego. She'd sooner brave a tornado. It would be safer by far.

She slipped Trace her hotel key, and kissed his cheek. Then she dove into the bushes and escaped.

* * * * *

What in the world had just happened?

Trace blinked. Now you see her, now you don't. He was beginning to lose touch with reality.

Yet the key in his fist felt very real. So did the fans who awaited Storm outside the arena, snapping pictures of him as if he was famous—those that hadn't given chase to the elusive star.

Protective instincts almost choked him. He growled and snarled, evolution regressing five thousand years. "No comment."

His patients would love this. He'd be the talk of the town for the next decade. Hopefully, the photos would be dark and blurry. He'd blame it on a double.

He didn't know what to expect when he reached Skye Blue's room. He snuck through the service entrance and up the service elevators. Then he scouted out her hallway, making sure it was clear.

He let himself into the dark room quietly and wondered if she was there. The drapes were pulled so that he couldn't see beyond the light that poured in from the hallway. Once he shut the door, he couldn't see a thing.

"Skye?" He listened intently for signs of life. The bed creaked and a nightlight glimmered to life, illuminating Skye Blue stretched out on the king-sized bed in scandalously sexy lingerie.

He drank in the vision of her greedily. Her ebony tresses cascaded down to her waist. Sequined-rimmed openings in the bodice bared her nipples, which beaded under his devouring gaze. They beckoned him to suckle them. A G-string barely covered her pussy.

Animal instincts ripped through him and his cock sprung to life.

She licked her glossy lips, poured chocolate syrup over one nipple and strawberry over the other, then crooked her finger at him.

He almost came just watching her, but he held back, wanting to bury himself inside her luscious folds. And he wanted to snack on her lush desserts.

"Choices, choices," he drawled, stretching his long length beside her on the mattress. The chocolate syrup gleamed in the dim light, the scent strong.

He flicked his tongue over it, teasing her, then unable to restrain himself, pulled it into his mouth and sucked hard.

She writhed against him, burying her fingers in his hair. She imprisoned his head against her, not that he minded being jailed.

His hands skimmed her lush form, then he spread his palms over her flat abdomen. His thumb massaged her clit, eager to know every lovely inch of her.

She dragged his head to her other breast and moaned when he tasted her.

Strawberry flavor burst in his mouth. "Exquisite." He nibbled the hard peak, playing with it before he sucked on it.

On fire, he slid a finger into her tight sheath.

She groaned and wriggled against his hand. Then she pulled away from him and licked her way down his chest, following the trail of hair that began just above his navel.

Shudders of delight rippled through him. The soft tongue trailed fire in its wake.

She growled and ripped open his slacks with her teeth, then pushed the restraining material off. She undressed him and then towered over him, passion smoldering in her eyes.

Anticipating the ride of his life, he rolled onto his back so she could slide down his shaft.

Mischief twinkled in her eyes and she reached for the butterscotch syrup on the nightstand. She held it high over him and drizzled the golden syrup over him, pouring a very liberal amount over his cock.

Sticky and cool, it coated him. He couldn't wait for her to feast on him as he had feasted on her.

He reached for the siren and lowered her G-string, letting his fingers glide over the feverish, satiny flesh. "So very beautiful. Any chance I can see your face without the paint?"

She tensed and dragged in ragged gulps of air. Her brow puckered and she scooted back on the bed.

He could swear fear flickered across her eyes. *Why?* She had nothing to fear from him.

She couldn't be scared of him or she wouldn't bring him to her room, bare her body, and let him fuck her.

Strange. Ahh.

Well, he wasn't crazy enough to think this was forever, however much he might dream otherwise. He'd take what she offered and savor it. He couldn't deal with the insanity of her life on a daily basis, physician or not. One taste of the crazed fans was more than enough for him.

This was probably their last time together.

"Come here. It doesn't matter." His curiosity paled in comparison to her need for anonymity. He pulled her into his arms and kissed her deeply. Their hearts raced against one another's.

He cradled her close to his heart until her heartbeat returned to normal. Frustration attacked him and he bristled. Some white knight he was, unable to slay her dragons.

Finally she offered her lips to him and he drank of her deeply, drowning in ecstasy. Bewitched, he couldn't drink his fill of the gorgeous nymph.

Her glorious hair wrapped about them like a spider's web, blocking out all but a twinkle of light.

She nestled between his legs, his full erection trapped between them.

When his lungs depleted of oxygen, he tore away from her lips. "Isn't it about time you clean up some of that syrup?"

Mirth curved her lips, swollen from his possession. Her eyes glazed with passion, as if she wanted to lick her way down on him to his fully aroused cock, but was concerned her makeup would rub off. Instead, she scooted down his length to capture the pearly drop of liquid glistening on the tip of his penis.

Convulsions hit him at the first lick of her tongue. Waves of pleasure coursed through him and he thrust into her mouth.

She sucked greedily, her fingers circling the base of his cock and stroking gently, milking him. Her other hand cupped his balls, gently kneading them.

Heaven couldn't be half so wonderful. He ground his hips against her, magnificent pressure building.

Seed exploded from his cock, overflowing her mouth. Voraciously, she continued to suck on him as she pumped him for more until he was drained.

Purring, she snuggled into his arms, molding herself to him.

Dreamily, he gazed upon her, rubbing her nipple between his fingers. "You like butterscotch, don't you?" *He'd never think of that flavor the same. Nor chocolate or strawberry.* They'd forever be linked to Skye Blue and this unforgettable night.

She nodded and pointed to him, her brows raised.

Ah, so she wanted to play charades again. His pulse raced again. "Pineapple. I'll bring some next time."

Next time? Her eyes widened in surprise. But she wasn't half as shocked as him. He hadn't planned that far ahead. He was taking this one moment at a time.

"Do you want there to be a next time?" *Maybe she didn't want to see him again.*

She gazed deeply into his eyes and nodded. Her fingertip circled the head of his cock and she kissed his chest.

What an appetite!

His cock sprang back to life. He was more than willing to quench it.

She rolled over and crawled onto her knees, wiggling her gorgeous ass in front of his face.

Raw need consumed him. A gentleman, he couldn't disappoint a lady. He rose behind her, slid his finger in and out to lubricate her first, and then rammed his cock into her tight sheath as far as she could take him. Amazingly, she swallowed almost all of him.

He massaged her clit as he slammed into her.

His breathing grew ragged, his blood sizzled and his heart somersaulted. His stomach clenched and semen built to explosive levels.

She moaned and gasped, grinding her pretty buttocks against him, begging to be fucked harder and faster. Their breathing became raw and heavy.

He exploded, holding her tightly, and he spewed his seed deep inside her as she writhed against him.

* * * * *

Trace woke up to a lonely hotel room. The only evidence to his lover's presence was the lingering scents of their incredible lovemaking that permeated the sheets that surrounded him.

He lay prone and gazed at the ceiling wondering if this had all been a fantastic wet dream. But no, his leather pants draped the dresser where Skye Blue had flung them in her frenzy.

He searched the hotel room, not surprised when he didn't find any other sign of her. Although she'd give him her body, she wouldn't give him anything else, not even a glimpse of her face.

Why was she so mysterious? The damned paparazzi probably. Or maybe she had a full-time thing with her band member and he was just a snack.

He'd never been a snack before and he didn't like it.

He showered, dressed, and marched down to the concierge. "Can you tell me the name of the lady in room 1410?" Impatient, he drummed his fingers on the counter.

"I'm afraid that's confidential information, Sir. I'm unable to divulge our hotel guests' private information."

It had been a long shot, but worth a try. Frustrated, he shoveled his fingers through his hair. "Thanks." For nothing.

Chapter Eight

Wendy kept her word and joined her sister at the Miss Weston pageant the next morning.

Shy of sleep, she suppressed several yawns. Trace's lovemaking had wiped her out physically. His questions had worn her out mentally.

She couldn't begin to understand how Angel and her competitors could prance before the vile photographers. Bile rose in her throat every time one of them batted a flirty lash. *Did they enjoy living in a fish bowl?*

"How's my hair look?" Angel peered into the mirror and sprayed a stray lock into place. "Not too stiff, is it?"

Wendy tried not to choke on the nasty aerosol shower as she evaluated her sister's immaculately groomed mane. "It looks good."

"Is it sleek and glossy? I want it to shine for the cameras." Angel wiggled around, adjusting the low-cut gown that insisted on falling further than decency permitted. Her cleavage threatened to spill out of the skimpy sequined bodice.

"Any glossier and it'll look greasy." Wendy grew hot when her thoughts flashed back to her own scandalous sequined bodice that had driven Trace crazy the previous night.

Angel gasped and held out a strand. Her chest rose and fell rapidly as she stared at it cross-eyed. "It's not greasy, is it? There's no time to wash and set it again.

Should I wear my wig? But what if it falls off mid-stage? I'd be laughed off-stage."

Wendy dropped her hands to her sister's shoulders and gave them a sisterly squeeze. "Relax. I didn't mean that. Your hair's perfect. Would you like me to spray a little glitter in it to jazz it up?"

Angel's lips curled in relief and she nodded. "Please. But not too much. I just want a little shimmer when the light catches it, not look like a Christmas tree."

Wendy was surprised to discover she was actually having fun. She hadn't fixed her sister's hair in almost a decade. In fact, she hadn't done much of anything with her sister in that long. She needed to remedy that, starting now. "Don't worry. I won't make you garish. Close your eyes."

She misted her sister's hair with the glitter, then stood back to study her handiwork. "You're angelic. No one else will hold a candle to you."

Except for her talent. Guilt ate at Wendy. She should have been coaching Angel on better breathing and vocal techniques. If the event wasn't for a few days, she might be able to impart a few tips. "When is the talent competition?"

"Tonight. Would you listen to me practice?" Angel warmed up her voice. "Me me me."

"Go through all the scales for me," Wendy said, putting on her teacher hat. Her voice coaches always made her warm up singing scales before striking out in song.

Angel cleared her throat and sang, "Do-re-mi-fa-so-la-ti-do."

Wendy tried not to wince at the flat, off-pitch notes. "Not bad, but let me hear it again. This time, go up an octave and hold the fa two beats longer."

Angel gave her a blank stare. "How do I know if I've gone up a whole octave?"

Wendy held her smile in place as she stifled an inward groan. They needed more time—at least a month. But she would do her best. "Is there a piano around here?"

"I don't know." Angel stood and fluttered about, wringing her hands together. "I suppose I'm screwing this up? Maybe I should just recite a dramatic poem."

Wendy hugged her, alarmed at how fast her sister's pulse raced. "Don't give up so fast. It wasn't bad. I was just giving you some pointers." Since there was no piano to give a middle C, Wendy did the next best thing. "Start with this note, like this." She sang, "Do re me fa so la te do."

Angel gaped at her, her kohl-rimmed eyes wide. "When did you learn to sing like that? If any of my competition does that, I'm doomed."

Clapping deafened her and stole her breath. She whirled around to find Trace leaning against the doorjamb, staring at her as if he'd never seen her before. One hand was behind his back. "Bravo. When did you learn to sing that way?"

Embarrassed, Wendy wanted to eat the notes. She had only sung the scales, not an opera, not even rock and roll. She cleared the frog out of her throat. "I took a few lessons as a kid. How long have you been there?"

"A couple of minutes. I didn't want to break the mood."

"Have you thought about singing or teaching voice for a living instead of selling hygiene products? It'd be a lot more fun if nothing else." Angel stared at her closely, also, as if she had shape-shifted into some alien creature.

Wendy tried to laugh away their high praise, but her insides churned. She was getting an awful case of indigestion. "Come on, guys. It was only the scales."

"Sing something else for us." Trace smiled at her encouragingly. He nodded to her and watched her raptly.

If there was any mercy in the world, the ground would open up and swallow her. The jig would be up the moment they heard her sing an actual song. It had been dangerous to sing anything. "I'm too shy. I'm just a shower singer."

Trace chuckled, a wicked glint in his eyes that boded no good. "Maybe we should put you in the shower and let you sing for us."

The perfumed air grew steamy and her heart raced. Did he want to get in that shower with her? Just what was he suggesting? "So you're still an incorrigible tease."

"Who said I'm teasing?" He straightened and swaggered over to her. He looked down on her from his great height, humor twinkling in his eyes.

God help her, but he still smelled like leather. The aroma of butterscotch had long fled or her bones would have melted to syrup. Her mouth watered for another sensual butterscotch sundae like they had shared the night before.

She shook herself mentally. If she didn't get her appetite under control, it would be the death of her. If only Trace didn't keep showing up in unexpected places, she might have a chance. He was like chocolates—she couldn't eat just one. Her mouth watered for more.

"Who let you in the dressing room?" His habit of showing up backstage began to irk her.

"I always come back to visit Angel and wish her well before her pageants." He brought out a bouquet of peach tinted roses from behind his back and held them out to Angel. "Go get 'em, tiger."

Wendy's heart dropped to her knees. He knew the exact color of her gown so that he could match the roses?

"Beautiful." She almost choked on the word and had to turn her back on him lest he read the heartache blazing in her eyes.

"Thank you, Trace! How gorgeous! They're absolutely divine." Angel leaned forward and slashed a kiss across his lips. To Wendy's consternation, her sister's breasts almost fell out of her dress.

"Beautiful petals for a beautiful flower." Trace's gaze simmered when presented with her sister's charms.

I'm going to be sick.

She shouldn't have come. He called her Freddie and her sister a beautiful flower. *No competition.*

Something was obviously going on between her sister and the doctor. Stars hovered before her eyes and she didn't know whether to be angrier that the cad was cheating on her sister with a rock singer, or to be jealous on her own account.

"I need a breath of fresh air. Excuse me." She had to escape now before the lovebirds made her gag. Angel couldn't fulfill all Trace's sexual desires or he wouldn't have visited her bed. Yet her sister would make the perfect trophy wife, just what the doctor ordered. What doctor didn't want a beauty queen for his bride? Her sister would look superb in his Lexus.

She marched to the exit and hung over the second story railing, inhaling deeply. She'd never felt this nauseous before a Storm concert. Why did Trace affect her so? She had burned for him as long as she could remember. She needed an exorcism, especially if he was to become her brother-in-law.

The door opened behind her and a whoosh of cold air chilled her back. Heavy footsteps warned her of another presence. "You okay?"

She breathed deeply and steeled herself against the two-timing lothario. The hair on the back of her neck stood on end. "I'm fine. I'm great. Why wouldn't I be?" Sarcasm dripped from her words, but she forced a chipper smile to her lips and turned around. She wouldn't be fine if she consumed a hundred pounds of chocolate.

"You rushed out of there like the room was on fire. Did I do or say anything to offend you?" He leaned against the wall and crossed his arms over his broad chest. His gaze bore into her. Deep creases puckered his forehead.

"Nothing." He had no love or affection for her. Just for Angel and Skye Blue, the womanizer.

He pushed himself off the wall with his foot and joined her at the railing. "So, why are we speaking in clipped monosyllables?"

She cursed him for stealing her breath, oozing such an abundance of testosterone it was about to asphyxiate her. "Why do you care? You're falling down on your job. You're supposed to be inside fawning over my sister." She turned her back on him again and leaned on the railing. She'd rather watch the alley cats maraud the garbage than look at his lying face.

"Whoa! Where did that come from? What nerve did I touch?" He turned and leaned over the railing, also, brushing her arm with his.

"My, aren't we the vain one? What makes you think you touched my nerves?" She glared at him, her nostrils flaring. Angel had an exclusive on him touching anything...at least her sister thought so.

"Do you mind speaking English? Let's back up. I took a wrong turn somewhere." Trace scowled and put a brotherly arm around her shoulders. "If it was the roses, I'd have brought you some, too, if I'd known you'd be here."

"So, you like threesomes?" Horrified, she couldn't believe that had come out of her mouth. Her acerbic mouth would be the death of her sooner rather than later.

An inscrutable expression masked his face and he crowded her into the corner, his breath hot on her neck, stoking her inner furnace to uncomfortable levels. "Do you?"

How did she get out of this one? Nothing came to mind, so she ducked under his arm and sprinted back inside to the soundtrack of his raucous laughter.

"You deserted me," Angel accused, pouting. "What hell hounds were chasing you?"

"I was just a little light-headed — all the hairspray, you know," Wendy lied, trying to regain her equilibrium. She looked pointedly at her watch. "When's showtime?"

"Showtime!" the plump, gray-haired stage mistress called from the doorway. She clapped her hands sharply, making Wendy jump.

Trace came in holding his ears, wincing. He clasped Wendy's elbow in his warm hand and tugged. "Come on, big sister. Our seats are getting cold."

He had two seats? "I thought you didn't know I'd be here."

"I imagine you have your mother's ticket. Mine is beside hers." His every stride swallowed two of hers, making her run to keep up. *Not very dignified.*

"Oh." Nor was her reply exactly eloquent, either. She was no Lennon with lyrics. Composing music was her forte. And singing.

"So, you want to try a threesome?" he mumbled against her ear as they made their way to the seats in the front center section.

"Shh!" Wendy would swear Trace was getting immense pleasure in embarrassing her. Very embarrassed, heat suffusing her cheeks, she murmured, "I never said that. Just drop it already."

"You're not getting off that easily. That did not come from the goody-two-shoes Freddie we all know and love."

She wished he loved her. At best, he thought of her as a kid sister...or future sister-in-law. Neither choice appealed to her.

"Whoever said I was a goody two-shoes?" She arched a brow at him. Of course, Thunder had called her anal and she hadn't kissed him till their fourth date. But she'd discovered butterscotch since then...

Her cheeks burned profusely at her wicked thoughts. It was a good thing he had the program open, covering his lap lest her gaze stray and he catch her checking out his assets.

She held her program up to hide her face, willing the heat to subside. The lights dimmed to her relief, and the music heralded the start of the program.

Breathtakingly beautiful women paraded onstage, her sister third in the procession. All flashed perfect teeth from exquisite faces. All boasted size two waists or smaller, modeling the most stunning ball gowns in the world. Angel was the most beautiful of the county's loveliest women, all of whom eclipsed Wendy ten times over with their beauty and elegance. Next to them, she was a toad.

She stared at the live Barbie dolls, her teenage insecurities flooding back. Her parents had valued her sister's physical beauty far above her own inner beauty and talent. They'd spent all their time and money parading Angel to beauty pageants up and down the state since before she could toddle. But there'd never been enough money or time to give Wendy voice lessons.

Angel had been their pride and joy. Gauche and plain, Wendy had been pushed to the side.

Trace elbowed her and whispered in her ear, "There she is, Miss America." He nodded at Angel who beamed at him radiantly.

"Yep. That's my sister, Miss America." Her voice didn't sound half as enthusiastic as Trace's. What had happened to her vow to mend the relationship with her sister? It was drowning in vain, stupid jealousy. She needed to get a grip. It wasn't as if she was without attributes or success. Still, the thought failed to comfort her when Trace's sultry gaze ravished her sister.

"She's really something, isn't she?" *What was Trace? President of Angel's fan club?* She had to know.

"Can I ask you a really personal question?" She twisted in her seat to look at him and rubbed elbows accidentally. Electric current charged her, making her jerk back.

Trace eyed her curiously, an indulgent expression etching his features. "What really personal thing could you want to know about me?"

She licked her suddenly dry lips. Now, that she was committed, she wasn't sure she wanted to know. "Are you planning to marry my sister? Do you love her?"

Trace's jaw dropped. He tensed and looked like a rabbit caught in her headlamps. "Whoa! You don't pull any punches. Did she put you up to this?"

"No. She'd probably kill me if she knew I was asking." She hid her trembling hands beneath her program and quelled her shivers. "So?"

"Why do you want to know? What is it to you?"

His counter-offense stung. "Just curious. I mean, you brought her roses to match her gown. You attend all her pageants. You haunt our house. I just wanted to know if I should be on the lookout for a bridesmaid's dress." She prayed not and hoped she sounded believable without sounding jealous.

"Uh huh." He leaned over her, his mischievous, questioning gaze, blazing into hers. "What really gives?"

She had to think fast or he'd know she was a complete fool about him. "You caught me. Mom put me up to it, not Angel. She's itching to be a grandmother, and I want her off my back."

"So, you have no plans to settle down and raise a family?"

If she couldn't have Trace, no. Not yet anyway, while the band was so hot and they were at the apex of their career. "I'm not going to settle for just anybody to please my mother, if that's what you mean."

"You've not met Mr. Right, then?"

She swallowed hard, not about to admit the truth, but neither willing to lie. "Let's just say I'm not ready yet, even if Mom is."

He patted her hand as if she was a little girl. "Rest assured your mother has many years left to see her grandchildren. There's no rush."

Her head ached from playing games with him. Trace wasn't any more willing than she to answer questions.

The procession ended and the contestants sang the state song and then the national anthem. She stood for the second and mouthed the words, too aware of Trace at her side.

"Guess you need a shower," he whispered in her ear as they were sitting down. His long leg brushed against hers, shooting sparks up her thigh.

"Excuse me?" She glared at him.

He frowned at her but chuckled. "I mean, you need a shower so you can sing."

She rolled her eyes at him. That was so ten minutes ago.

Next, Angel glided onstage to show off her gown. Light reflected off her sequins as she swayed gracefully down the runway. Posing regally, she smiled at the audience, and gave the queen's wave.

Tortured, Wendy snuck veiled glances at Trace, who seemed mesmerized by her sister. What had she done to deserve this punishment? She prayed her mother recovered quickly so she could remove herself from this torment.

"So beautiful," he murmured, his gaze rapt on Angel.

"Yes." Wendy couldn't argue. Couldn't Trace see past the skin deep perfection?

Unfortunately, he wasn't alone. Thunder had learned to his detriment that physical beauty alone didn't make for a good marriage. Or even a good conversation. *Last time she checked, however, it wasn't her job to educate the world to the evil of empty-headed Barbie dolls. Thunder reaped what he had sown.*

Graceful, Angel didn't stumble once. Her smile didn't falter. The light radiated off the sparkles in her hair. She was crowned Miss Weston USA.

Wendy jumped and cheered, sticking her fingers in her mouth and whistling her glee. Joy and despair battled inside. Pride swelled in her heart.

* * * * *

"Congratulations, sweetheart. I knew you could do it." Bessie fawned over Angel, twittering all weekend long. "I'm so proud of you, baby girl. You've done right by the family. You're on your way to the big time. We have to get busy finding more sponsors for you."

After a solid weekend of the gushing and fawning, Wendy couldn't take one more compliment and escaped to the solitude of her mother's butterfly sanctuary to help weed it, as her mother had been unable to tend to it since her collapse. Several species of butterflies flitted around. She remembered most of them, but there were a few new varieties she'd have to look up.

A zebra butterfly landed on her outstretched finger and fluttered its wings. Peace settled over her, and she breathed in the beautiful flowery essence around her. This was her favorite part of her home, the best of her mother.

After an hour or so, she powered down her cell phone, curled up on the bench, and caught a nap.

"There you are." Trace's husky voice broke through her sleep. "Your mother is out of her mind with worry thinking you fell into the canal or got kidnapped."

Wendy sat up, stretched and yawned. "What time is it?" She'd forgotten to put on her watch, but judging from the sun's position, it must be afternoon.

"About four-thirty. They've been looking for you for hours, sleeping beauty. You missed lunch." Trace sat beside her on the bench and turned to watch her. "This is quite a place, isn't it?"

"Four-thirty!" Adrenalin surged through her. "I've been asleep since after we got back from the pageant." She dashed inside, then stopped dead in front of the dining room table when she saw Skye Blue's face and Trace's staring up at her from the cover of a glossy tabloid.

Trace ran into her back, and she pitched forward. He reached out and grabbed her before she would have banged into the table's sharp edge. He held her against him as they caught their breath.

"Did you see this?" Her heart skipped a few beats and she paled. Then to cover her faux pas, she added, "That looks just like you. It could be your double." The cameras had caught Trace's full face on film before she'd been able to hide him. *Damn damn damn!*

Trace released her and picked up the magazine, grimacing. "Damn!" Bristling, he echoed her sentiments. Opening the magazine to the article, he scanned it.

Angel sauntered into the room, her curious gaze studying the photograph. "Is that you? Everyone is saying so."

Wendy's heart went out to Trace. Butterflies filled her stomach. She didn't trust her voice to sound innocent.

"You know Skye Blue?" Angel thrust out her chest and anchored her hands on her hips.

"We've met," he admitted grudgingly as if it left a bad taste in his mouth.

"Since when do you wear leather? The two of you look pretty cozy. Just how well do you know her?" Angel narrowed her eyes at Trace.

"I've only met her a couple of times. No big deal." Boredom rang in Trace's voice. But his eyes flashed fire.

No big deal... The sentiment echoed in Wendy's head and squeezed her heart. *So, that's how he felt.*

"Well, don't go kissing the wild woman. She might be contagious." Bessie ambled out of her bedroom and grabbed the paper away from Trace. "Let me see that." After perusing the magazine for a moment, she rolled it up and slapped it into his open palm. "That one's 100% slut. You're too good for the likes of her. What head are you thinking with, son?"

Angel nodded her head sharply, punctuating their mother's words.

Contagious? Slut? Desolate, her heart aching, Wendy digested their nasty comments. Now, she knew for sure what her family thought of her. Seething, she waved her hand, pivoted on her heel, and left the room. *She was so out of there.*

Fuming, Wendy muttered all the way back to her room. When she reached it, Trace caught up to her, grabbed her arm, and spun her around to face him. "Why did you storm off like that?"

She shook off his offending hand and glared up at him, clenching and unclenching her fists. Her blood raged in her veins. "You're a creep, that's why."

"Why? Because I know Skye Blue? Because I was caught in a photograph with her? Where do you come off passing judgment on my personal life?"

"Nowhere. Absolutely nowhere."

"What's that supposed to mean?"

"Take it anyway you like. You will anyway." She tried to duck under his arm and escape into her room, but he blocked her.

Questions lit his eyes and he rubbed his chin. "What am I missing here? Why are you mad at me?" He changed subtly and leaned over her, a predatory gleam in his eyes. "Are you jealous?"

"That's absurd." How could she be jealous of herself?

Sometimes you are jealous of Skye Blue. Her scowl deepened as she tried to shut up her unwelcome, nagging conscience.

"Why is it so absurd? Do you find me so revolting that you never once thought about you and me?"

"You and me...what?" Her traitorous body betrayed her. Her eyes grew big and wide. Her lungs refused to exhale. Her knees grew wobbly, threatening to buckle.

Trace leaned closer so that his lips hovered mere inches from hers, so that his breath mingled with her suddenly heavy breaths. "Doing things men and women do together. Like kissing."

Before his words sank in, he captured her lips and parted them with his tongue. Ravenously, as if he hadn't kissed a woman for years, he plundered her mouth, drinking deeply. His arms crept around her, dragging her close, molding her to his lithe frame.

Electricity flared, igniting a fire in her core. She whimpered, wanting to push him away and wanting to nestle closer into his arms. *And she wasn't a split personality, right.*

Her lips stopped listening to reason and kissed him back hungrily, parting wide so that her tongue could mate with his. Surely he would recognize her from her kiss, from the way she fit into his arms so perfectly. The charade was over.

Finally, after all the fight in her had drained out, he released her lips, dragging in air deeply. He kissed her forehead, letting his lips linger on her feverish flesh seductively. "That's what I mean. You enjoyed it."

Some of the joy fled at his words. She wasn't sure how to take him. "I find kissing pleasurable, if that's what you mean."

"I mean, you find kissing me pleasurable."

"Not bad." She wasn't ready to confess undying, ever-after love. She wanted him to make the first declaration, let her know he recognized her or that he loved her, not Skye Blue. So far, he'd not reassured her of either.

His brow arched. "That's it. Not bad?"

What, she was supposed to admit his kisses sent her reeling over the moon? When she had no idea what his reaction would be?

"Am I supposed to invite you into my bed now?" How she wished she could, but not until she knew he wasn't just playing with her. "What would Skye Blue think if she knew you were kissing other women?"

His gaze smoldered on her, then on her bed. "Why would Skye have any say over me?"

"And what about Angel? What would she say if she knew about this?"

"Why should Angel say anything? We're just friends."

"Friends...like you and me?" Kissing friends? Bedroom friends?

"One kiss and now, there's a 'you and me'?" Heat roiled off him. Challenge flashed in his eyes as he straightened to his full height.

"Okay, explain to me what just happened here." He had to be the most frustrating man Wendy had ever met. And she had to be a masochist to burn for him for so many years.

"That's what I'd like for you to tell me. I'm waiting." He crossed his arms over his chest and rocked back on his worn heels.

Obviously, he couldn't add two plus two. Her secret was still safe, much to her chagrin. But she wasn't going to teach him how to add. "Bastard! You're just collecting scalps. First my sister. Then Skye Blue. Now me. You must think you're God's gift to women."

He blinked as if he'd been slapped. "I told you nothing ever happened with your sister..."

"I overheard the two of you years ago."

"We were kids. Nothing's happened since we've been adults."

"Yet you go to all her pageants? You give her roses?"

"She's like my little sister. You're family. I spent more time here growing up than I did in my own house."

"Do you always kiss your sisters that way?"

"Did I say that I look upon you like a sister? You've been gone a long time."

Okay, so he didn't view her as his sister. That wasn't all bad. But it didn't mean anything necessarily, either. "And Skye Blue? What about her?" She held her breath, hoping he would say what she longed to hear, fearing he wouldn't.

"None of your business."

If he only knew. "Why did you kiss me that way?" Obviously not because he knew she was Skye Blue.

"I felt like it. Do I need more reason? Can't we just let it go at that? I'm not in the habit of explaining who I kiss or why."

"Fine!" She was such a bigger bitch than Skye Blue who just went with the flow and let him do whatever he liked to her. "So, let it go already." She waved him away, dove into her room, and slammed the door. Her chest heaving, she locked her door, leaned against it, and slunk to the floor. He didn't love her or Skye Blue. He was just a player.

* * * * *

Whew! That she-devil wasn't the Freddie he remembered. He stared at the door several long moments, shoveling his hand through his hair. Freddie had always been high-strung, even moody, but never that big a witch. Her tongue had grown rapier sharp to the point of being deadly. *For Heaven's sake, it was only a little kiss.*

Well, that little kiss had rocked his world, and stars had fallen from the sky, but he'd not pledged his allegiance to her or anything so monumental. He hoped she wasn't one of those women who thought one kiss obligated him to life-long commitment. He wasn't sure where his heart lay.

No kiss had ever shattered him so, and it was one of the things that confused him. Freddie's kiss had been as explosive as Skye Blue's, shocking the hell out of him. And Freddie was a real woman, not some wild, mysterious, out-of-reach fantasy.

Unfortunately, she was also a woman in a really bad mood. Why was she so pissed at him? He hadn't done anything except steal a kiss...or have his picture taken with the diva. Could she be jealous of the rock star? Did she feel more for him than she was willing to admit? She had grown into a fascinating woman.

Another, less palatable thought made him scowl. Maybe she didn't want him touching her because she was already involved in another relationship. Mr. Hair practically growled at him as if he was invading his territory. But if that was the case, he hadn't minded the half-naked babes oohing and aahing over his muscles at the health spa. Maybe Freddie should be warned about her roving-eyed boyfriend.

He chased his patient back to bed, glad that she was getting stronger, but mourning the fact that this meant Freddie's stay was coming to an end. She had made no secret of the fact that she was out of here as soon as her mother had regained her health. Bessie's vitals were strong enough she'd outlive the mighty oaks. It wouldn't hurt Bessie to rest a few more days while he sorted out his feelings. Nor would it hurt Freddie to unwind a little. She was strung much too tightly. That job of hers was no good for her.

He spied Freddie climbing into Mr. Hair's car as he exited the house, and swore. He couldn't see what she saw in that longhaired hippie. No real man would be caught dead looking like Lady Godiva. If he hadn't seen it with his own eyes, he wouldn't have believed that Freddie could be attracted to such an effeminate man.

He followed them to the next town and watched them go into a house together, laughing. He swore again and punched the dashboard. He asked himself the question of the century, why did he even care?

Chapter Nine

"You're going to dig this." Lightning chuckled wryly and passed a hated tabloid to Wendy. He snarled as if he didn't love what he was handing to her.

Grimacing, Wendy waved the paper away and plopped into a kitchen chair. "I've seen that nasty thing. I don't want to see it again." The scrambled eggs made her stomach grumble, so she scooped a portion onto her plate and snatched a slice of toast from the center of the table. Thunder slid a cup of espresso to her and she took a grateful sip.

"So, what are you going to do about it? They've really overstepped their bounds this time. I'd sue." Lightning bit into a stacked ham sandwich and then licked mayonnaise off his lips.

"It's just a picture of me with Trace. I'm not thrilled but it's nothing to sue over." She spread light margarine on her toast and then munched on it as she regarded her friends lounging around the table.

"This is something else. You mustn't have seen it yet." Lightning slid it back to her, the veins in his hand bulging.

Thunder leaned over her shoulder, grabbing for the paper.

She batted his hand away, then spluttered out her coffee across the table when she read the headline. "Skye Blue Caught in Lesbian Love Nest?" Photographs of Skye Blue and herself seemed to jump off the page. Thank God the picture of her without makeup was dark, and grainy. *She was being accused of having a lesbian relationship with herself? Had they followed Trace to her room that night? Or did it mean that the press had hidden outside her hotel room door to get those pictures?* "I'm going to throw up."

Lightning wiped coffee off his arm.

Thunder chuckled. He gathered his darts and set up his dartboard, one of his favorite past times. "Well, luv, this means you'll have to come out of the closet."

Wendy twisted around and punched him in the shoulder. "You know I'm not a lesbian."

"One way or another, you'll have to come out. Guess we all will." Thunder balanced a dart in his hand, took aim, and tossed it into the air. It nearly hit the bull's eye.

"This could be really fantastic promo if handled right. It'll be the biggest news since the OJ Trial." A thoughtful expression flitted across Hail's face.

Wendy couldn't believe her ears. "You want to turn our lives into a publicity stunt? Don't you care what this will do to us?"

"You're the only one who's not come clean with your family. We warned you this could happen anytime." When Wendy quirked her brow, Thunder's eyes twinkled and he added quickly, "Well, not the lesbian part."

"So, how and when do we go public?" Hail tapped her collagen-filled lips with her finger. "It should be a big splash."

"We should milk this for all the publicity we can, first." Lightning eyed her speculatively. "That Brittney/Madonna thing is big news. Why shouldn't we cash in on some free publicity, too?" He wiggled his finger at Wendy and Hail. "How about the two of you …you know?"

Wendy stuck her tongue out at the incurable tease. "I can't believe you'd even jest about that. Publicity isn't king. You know what this'll mean?"

Thunder massaged her shoulders with his magic fingers. "That your boyfriend will find out you've been scamming him? That Mommy Dearest and Miss Universe will find out you're not the world's champion hygiene saleswoman?"

Wendy glared up at him. "That's not precisely how I would've put it, but I do need time to clear the record with them before we come out of the closet."

"You know, Rog and Celia should be in on this conversation. We need to plan a big campaign. A coming out party." Rain scribbled notes on a small pad of paper.

"You're such a diva bitch. I'm way ahead of you, sister." Hail was already dialing her cell phone.

"Maybe we can get a gig on Oprah. And Jerry Springer." Rain, the big thinker, dreamed aloud. She started making a list of all the talk shows that thrived on scandals and dysfunctional families.

"Maybe we can call our next album 'Coming Out of the Closet'? And we can show our real faces?" Hail's eyes gleamed. She twirled her hoop earring, then murmured into the phone.

Rain rubbed her splotchy crimson cheeks. "Yeah, I'm sick of all that makeup. It's giving me a rash. My dermatologist is buying his Mercedes on my makeup."

"But the painted faces are our calling card." Wendy shuddered at the thought of singing in front of thousands of people without her disguise. Her mask lent her courage. "I can't face our fans out of costume."

"Sure you can, luv. I'll be at your side." Thunder worked his way up her neck and caressed her earlobe.

She wrenched away and batted at his hand. "You're forgetting one little thing…your wife."

Thunder grinned unabashed and flashed his dazzling teeth. "I said I'll be with you on stage, not fucking you."

Wendy gasped and threw a piece of toast at him. "You wicked, vile man."

Thunder bowed low, his glorious mane of golden hair cascading to the floor. "You know you love me."

"Don't egg him on. He lives to pull your chain." Lightning's grin flashed also. He downed his cup of espresso, then wiped his mouth with the back of his hand.

"It's so easy to pull." Thunder straightened up laughing.

"What is this? Pick on Wendy day?" She glowered at the men, wishing she'd joined an all-girl band.

Thunder hugged her. "You know we love you."

"You can stop sucking up. You know that no one else would put up with you deviants." Wendy stood and dumped her food in the garbage and washed her plate.

"She loves us," Lightning said to Thunder. "I don't know how much more adoration I can stand."

Wendy's cell phone buzzed in her pocket, tickling her thigh. She sighed and dragged it out.

"Three guesses," Thunder purred from his perch on the breakfast nook's bench. "Mommy Dearest calling you home for dinner?"

She stood and mumbled, "I'll just take this in private." She locked herself in the bathroom so Thunder couldn't follow. That was all she needed was for her mother to overhear his warped sense of humor and take offense. Bessie was already an expert at jumping to conclusions without that kind of help.

Thunder was psychic. It was her mother. Tears choked her voice. "Dear, supper's almost ready and we were wondering if you'd be joining us tonight? It's your father's and my anniversary, and you know how I like for the entire family to be together on this day. It helps me forget how lonely I am."

How could she have forgotten her parent's anniversary? "Of course I'll come right home. I just have to say goodbye."

"Oh? To whom?"

"Ian." She didn't feel like elaborating. She frowned at herself in the mirror and scrunched her nose.

"Is that the young man with all the hair? He's back?"

"Yes, he's back."

"Why don't you invite him to dine with us tonight? I'd really like to meet him. I don't know any of your friends anymore." Bessie paused strategically. "Or is he more than a friend? Do I hear wedding bells?"

Her head began to ache and she rubbed it. "I don't think he'll be able. He has other plans…"

"Put him on the phone."

"Wh-what?"

"You heard me, dear. Put your friend Ian on the phone. I want to speak to him."

"He's not in the room."

"Is he in the house? Nearby?" Her mother's voice became more insistent and wheedling.

"Well, yeah…"

"Go get him and put him on the phone." Command rang decisively in her mother's voice. Wendy knew better than to argue with Bessie when she took on this tone.

She went in search of Thunder and thrust the phone out to him robotically. "Mom wants to speak to you, Ian."

Thunder's brows rose, but he took the phone. "Ian here. It's so nice to finally meet you, Mrs. Applegate. Wendy's raved about how wonderful you are." He went on to charm her mother, adopting the tone of a long-lost best friend.

The rest of the band tried to stifle their laughter behind their hands and she glared at them. Predicting gloom and doom, she hung her head. Nothing good could come of this. *One didn't dump gasoline on fire and expect to put out the flames.*

"I'd be delighted to join you for dinner tonight. No, no. You're not taking me away from any plans."

Lightning smirked. "We need to practice, you moron. The Key West concert is this weekend and you two barely know the lyrics to the new songs."

Thunder covered the receiver with his hand and put his finger to his lips. "Yes, we'll come right away. Promise, luv."

Thunder snapped the phone shut and tossed it to Wendy. "Move your buns, Fred. Your lovely mother awaits her anniversary dinner." To Lightning and the girls, he tossed over his shoulder, "We'll be back later to practice."

"Promises. Promises. I won't hold my breath." Lightning strummed the exit march on his guitar, a mock glare in his eyes.

That's all she could seem to do—hold her breath. When they were out of eyeshot of their friends, Wendy grasped Thunder's wrist. "Promise me you won't say anything about Storm or Skye Blue. I want to tell them in my own way. I'm not ready yet."

"Anything you say, luv." Thunder held the car door wide for her, humming happily.

She didn't trust him when he was being too compliant. She looked at his hands for signs of poison apples. She coached him on her cover during the journey. "You got that?"

"They're your family. Just tell them now, before it comes out in some worse way." Thunder patted her hand.

"My family thinks Skye Blue is a slut." *A contagious slut.*

"Bummer. Still, they have to be told."

"I'll come clean after the Miss Florida pageant. I don't want to upstage Angel's big moment."

"And when is that?"

"In two weeks."

"I don't know if we can keep the lid on for two weeks. For all we know, some photographer has us in his sights now. Skye Blue's hot news." Thunder looked in the rear view mirror pointedly.

She gasped and twisted around in her seat to peer out the rear window. "Is someone following us?"

"Not that I can see, but I'm keeping my eyes open."

Chills crept up her spine. "Why can't people mind their own business?"

"Because it doesn't work that way. Their lives are dull, so they get their excitement making us squirm by making up stories, like that Skye Blue lesbian thing." He pulled into the driveway and parked next to Trace's Lexus.

She closed her eyes and mumbled to herself, "Heaven help me."

"Come on. Your mother sounds like an absolutely lovely woman and if she's anything like her daughter, I'm sure she's very charming." Thunder opened her door and escorted her to the house.

Wendy bared her teeth and growled at him. "Don't count on it. Promise me you'll behave." She wouldn't be surprised if her mother chased him with a pair of barber shears.

Before he could promise, her mother rushed outside in her best church finery and pearls. "Welcome, welcome! I'm Bessie, Wenefred's mother. It's so nice to finally meet you. Wenefred's never brought a man home before."

Wendy scrunched up her face. Next, her mother would be showing off her naked baby pictures.

Thunder bowed low and kissed her mother's hand. "The pleasure's all mine."

"What beautiful hair you have." Bessie admired it as she ushered them in.

Was this the same woman who called him 'Mr. Hair' and bemoaned the fact he looked like a hippy?

Trace and Angel were deep in debate.

Her mother's prize china and crystal graced the table. The succulent aroma of a steaming roast made her stomach grumble.

Thunder stopped short and bristled when he spied Trace.

No better, Trace's nostrils flared when he looked up and caught sight of Thunder.

Wendy swallowed a sigh, took Thunder's hand, and led him over to Trace and her sister. Dread clawed at her. How did she introduce the other man? 'I'd like to formally introduce you to the man you propositioned for a threesome when he was making love to me! Maybe you don't recognize him from the front, but I'm sure you would if he were to drop his pants and let you see his backside.'

She didn't think that would go over very well, so she substituted, "Ian, I'd like you to meet my sister Angelina. I'd also like to introduce you to our next-door neighbor, Trace Cooper. Angel just won the title of Miss Weston USA and she'll be going on to the Miss Florida pageant in a couple weeks. Trace is also my mother's doctor."

Ian squeezed her hand so painfully tight she had to bite back a wince. "And I'd like you to meet my best friend, Ian Keith. He's a fellow sales rep for our company."

Interest lit Angel's eyes as her gaze raked over Thunder's attributes. "Do you sell feminine hygiene products, too?" she asked sweetly.

Thunder flashed a smile guaranteed to make red-blooded females melt at his feet. He'd had a lot of practice on his adoring fans, but Angel didn't have her antibodies against his deadly allure. "Condoms, luv. I sell rubbers. We specialize in the flavored, neon glowing ones."

She would get him for this. She tapped her fingers against her leg.

To her horror, he grabbed her hand and put it on his butt, then dragged her against his side and held her close. "She can't keep her hands off me. We're just wild about each other."

Trace's face became an inscrutable mask.

Wendy wrestled away from her ex-best friend and glared at him. "We're just good friends."

Thunder shrugged and grinned secretively. "If you say so, luv."

Bessie smiled radiantly at her and Thunder. "Might I hear wedding bells in the future?"

When she opened her mouth to state an emphatic 'No!' Thunder cast a possessive arm about her shoulders and interrupted, "You never know."

Wendy elbowed him hard in the ribs. "I do know. We're just friends."

Thunder put his hands over his heart and gazed at her meltingly. "Tear out my heart."

"Call us when dinner's ready." Leaving Thunder alone with her family, and especially with Trace, was too dangerous, so she dragged him with her to the butterfly sanctuary.

She whirled around and faced off against him. "What do you think you're doing? Should I kick your butt all the way to next week?"

"I wasn't lying in there." Thunder got down on bended knee before her and clasped her hand. Butterflies twittered around them.

"Get up!" she hissed, mortified. "What are you doing down there? What if someone sees you?"

"I don't care if the whole world sees me. I love you and want you to be my wife. Marry me, Wendy." He kissed her hand and gazed up at her with big puppy dog eyes.

"Are you daft?"

"Not exactly the response I dreamed of, luv."

"You're already married. What response did you expect?"

"That can be remedied. Just say the word and Carly's history. We both know I should have married you. I love you."

"We don't both know anything of the sort. I love you but ..."

Trace cleared his throat, cutting off her 'as a brother'. His eyes narrowed on her. "Dinner's ready. Your mother sent me to fetch you."

Her heart stopped beating and she couldn't breathe. *Had he heard them?* She scowled at her friend and ordered again, "Get up."

She joined Trace. Licking her lips, she asked, "What did you hear?"

"Enough to know you're engaged to Mr. Hair. I mean Ian."

She placed a hand on his arm, dismayed at its stiffness. "I'm not engaged to Ian anymore."

Trace turned to look at her. "Anymore? You said you were just friends."

"We are now. He broke the engagement a couple of years ago."

"He did? And now he's seen the error of his ways and wants you back. Congratulations. You must be ecstatic." He plucked her hand off his arm and sat between her mother and Angel, effectively cutting her off.

Was she mute? Invisible? Why did no one listen to her? She swirled the water in her crystal goblet, watching the ice melt, and ignored her unpalatable food.

"How long have you known one another?" Bessie asked, staring dreamily at Thunder. She forked a piece of beef and raised it to her lips.

Thunder looked thoughtful. "Oh, we go back a long way—about ten years."

Angel dropped her knife and it clattered against her plate. Her jaw flexed. "Ten years! And you've never mentioned him or introduced us?"

Thunder slid her an 'I-told-you-so' look.

"How were you together?" Bessie's sharp gaze pierced her.

"He sells flavored, neon condoms," Trace said dryly.

"We were engaged for awhile," Thunder said simultaneously.

Wendy choked on a swallow of water and started coughing again. She kicked her friend's shin.

"And you're not now?" Bessie turned and frowned at her. "Why didn't you tell me? So, you cut us all the way out of your life?"

Thunder nudged her knee with his and shot her a knowing look. He leaned close and whispered. "This would be the opportune time to come clean."

She couldn't push the words out of her throat and shook her head. "Not till after the Miss Florida pageant," she whispered back. In particular, not till after she had a chance to speak to Trace alone.

Bessie stabbed another piece of roast and waved it in the air. "Speak up or wait till you're alone to whisper."

"No secret, really," Wendy lied, crossing her fingers under the table.

"Speaking of secrets," Angel leaned forward and lowered her voice to a conspiratorial undertone, "did you see that Skye Blue was caught in a lesbian love nest?"

Wendy clenched her fingers around the stem of her goblet so tightly, it was a wonder she didn't snap it in two. Her fingernails dug painfully into the soft flesh of her palm. Otherwise, she couldn't exhale as her rapt gaze remained glued on Trace who tensed.

"We heard," Thunder said, and shoveled more potatoes into his mouth as if the revelation was of little consequence.

"Well? Can you believe it?"

Wendy finally found her voice. "Who says it's true?"

"They have pictures of her lover coming out of her room." Malicious glee glowed from Angel's eyes.

"Just coming out of the room? Together? Doing anything more incriminating than that?" *Since when was it a crime to walk in or out of a hotel room?*

"They have an eyewitness who swears she saw them kissing. I mean deep tongue, soul kissing."

Thunder tented his brow at her. "I'd like to see that."

Wendy dug her nails into her friend's thigh under the table.

"Ow!" Thunder yelled and jerked away from her.

Bessie lifted her chin and looked down her nose at Trace. "I told you that wild woman was not for you. You should have snagged my Wenefred when you had the chance. Angelina's still available…"

"Ian and I are not engaged," Wendy said through gritted teeth, slamming the table with the flat of her hand. China rattled, water spilled, and silverware jumped from the force.

Conversation hushed and all eyes turned on her making Wendy's blood ice over.

"Are you offering yourself up to me now?" Scowling, Trace wadded up his linen napkin and tossed it on top of his plate. He hitched up his slacks, stood, and pushed his chair against the table. He bent and kissed her mother on the cheek. "Bessie, I'm sorry but I have to run. I forgot I have to visit a patient at the hospital. I hope you enjoy the rest of your anniversary. Take it easy. You're still recovering, don't forget."

"I hope we didn't upset you about anything, old chap." Thunder continued to eat as if they were discussing nothing more controversial than the weather. Light from the dining room chandelier glinted off his glorious hair when he moved.

"I'll check in on you tomorrow. Let the girls clean this up and go rest," Trace said to her mother.

"Ciao." Thunder fluttered his fingers at Trace who didn't respond except to let the screen door slam behind him.

Wendy cringed and chased after Trace as he marched home. "Wait!" Panting, she caught up to him outside.

"I'm really not in the mood. So, if you'll excuse me." He reached for his door but she stepped in front of it, blocking his escape.

"Please don't be angry with me. I didn't say anything against your..." *What was she supposed to call herself?* "Friend."

"Angelina and your fiancé made some vicious insinuations." Fury boiled in his eyes.

"I don't have a fiancé but if it helps at all, I'm sorry they were being so unkind." She lowered her lashes and veiled her eyes. Now, how to ask the million-dollar question. "You must really like this Skye Blue, I mean, to get so upset like this." Or he might really think she was having an affair with herself.

"What's it to you whether or not I like her?" He backed her against the door and tilted her chin up so that his smoldering gaze pierced her. "Maybe you liked my kisses better than you let on? Maybe you're jealous?"

Her pulse raced and a sheen of perspiration broke out on her lip. "What if I am?" She could answer a question with a question as well as he could. She tried not to shiver from the electric current pulsing through her, but it was a tall order.

Finally, after an interminable pause, he narrowed his eyes. "I'd say you don't know your mind."

She crossed her arms over her chest. "Weren't you the one who said we shouldn't analyze everything to death? Take things as they come?"

"More or less." He cupped her face in his hands and plundered her lips with a searing kiss.

The universe spun dizzily and she drowned in bliss. She tangled her fingers in his thick, luxuriant hair and pressed her body to his. When his arousal pressed against her belly, tingles skipped down her spine and settled between the juncture of her legs.

Oxygen starved, she broke the kiss and nibbled his lower lip. Then she leaned her forehead against him and slid her hands up his chest. "That was nice."

He caressed her face. "More than nice. Maybe we should have tried this a long time ago."

"Probably." She inhaled deeply, screwing up her courage. She needed to tell him the truth and she wanted to fill him in before she confessed to her family lest they break the news to him in their usual undiplomatic fashion. "I really need to talk to you. Privately. Can I come inside?" Her voice came out sultrier than she had anticipated.

"You want to talk to me. Now?" Trace glanced around.

"Yes. Like in a conversation. I have something important to discuss with you." She gazed deeply into his eyes, wishing she could see into his soul. *How would he handle the truth?*

"Now?"

She nodded seductively and trailed a finger down his throat. "You don't really have a patient to check on, do you?"

He shifted uneasily. "Well, no. I just had to get out of there before I murdered someone for ridiculing Skye..." He stopped short and his eyes darkened. "Does it bother you that I have a relationship with her?"

She licked her lips. "No. But I would like to talk about it. It's important."

A shutter closed over his face. "I prefer not to."

"You might be surprised." Might be? Shocked was more like it. Very shocked.

"There you are, Wenefred." Thunder bounded down her mother's porch steps two at a time, and made a beeline for her. "I thought I'd lost you."

She tossed him her sweetest smile and crooked her head, grinding her teeth at the use of her hated name. "You can't lose what you don't have."

Thunder stepped back. "Ouch. Pull in your claws, sweetheart. I'm not the enemy."

Trace glared at him then swung his gaze back to her. "When you decide what it is you want, call me. Maybe we'll talk." Surprising her, he dove into his car and sped off. Red dust spewed behind him until all she could see was a cloud of powder.

She reeled on her friend, anchoring her hands on her hips. "You have lousy timing. And if you call what you did in there helping me, you're crazier than I thought."

"I love it when you talk dirty to me, luv."

She gave him a gentle shove as she trudged back to the house. Scuffling shells with the toe of her shoe, she ambled slowly home. "Dream on."

"I was serious about everything I said earlier." His expression sobered and he blocked her way. "I love you. What Carly and I have is a sham. It's not a real marriage. The only woman I think about is you, day and night."

Pity swelled in her heart. She knew how unrequited love felt and she didn't want to put her friend through it. Neither could she live a lie. "I don't love you in that way."

Thunder grabbed her hand and dragged it to his lips, nuzzling her knuckles. Although his lips were soft and warm against her flesh, they didn't shoot sparks through her. "Marriage is based on many things. Love is only one of them. We're partners. Best friends. We're in synch."

"Love's the most important part." She'd rather stay single than marry the wrong man. Much as she loved Thunder as a brother, much as she thought she'd loved him once, he wasn't right for her. She wasn't on fire for him. She wanted more out of marriage than he could give. They'd make each other miserable.

"You'll learn to love me that way. You used to. You can again. I'll make you love me."

Her smile faded. She felt stifled and lifted her heavy hair off her feverish neck to allow the soft evening breeze to cool her off. "I'm in love with Trace. I have to see where that leads."

"To disaster if you don't come clean. Next, the tabloids will have you sleeping with cattle."

She had been going to tell him now, until Thunder had chased him away.

Her heart lifted and she chuckled. If he could joke like that, he wasn't totally destroyed.

"See, I'm good for you. Admit it."

She tucked her arm through the crook of his and leaned against him. "I admit it. You're good for me. Just not as a husband."

"We can live together. I'm easy." He leaned his head against hers as they strolled companionably inside.

"I'd only disappoint you in the long run...I don't like threesomes." Her thoughts turned back to Trace and how she, Wendy, could seduce him. She needed to talk to him.

Chapter Ten

Trace pressed weights, and then swam laps until the health spa kicked him out at closing time. His tight muscles ached from the workout as his thoughts whirled around Wendy and Skye Blue.

He strode through the inky black parking lot to his car, swinging his gym bag. Damp hair fell across his eyes and he shoved it back with a grimace. He cursed the fact that all it took was a thought about either woman to make him go hard or his heart to race out of control. Swimming with a hard-on wasn't on his list of favorite things to do. His swimming trunks didn't exactly hide his erection. How could two such polar opposite women attract and confound him? He obviously didn't know his own mind or heart.

Wendy confused him most of all. Skye Blue was acting true to her wild woman image, although he wasn't sure what to make of the latest scandal. Still, she lived in the fast lane where most anything went. Wendy, on the other hand, was the wholesome girl-next-door.

At least she used to be. She had been engaged to marry that longhaired, condom-peddling hippy whom she still hung out with irregardless of his wife. She stayed out all night, usually with Mr. Hair, and disappeared every weekend. *The woman didn't make sense.*

When he pulled into his driveway, he frowned. Flickering lights illuminated his dining room window.

Fire!

Breathing hard, he slammed on the brakes and ran for the house. He dialed for emergency help on his cell phone as he stormed in the door and darted to the fire extinguisher. Hopefully, the blaze wasn't out of control yet.

Fire extinguisher in hand, his finger on the trigger, he entered the dining room...and stopped dead. Hundreds of flickering candles illuminated the room. Jasmine permeated the air. And a nearly naked Wendy lounged seductively on his sofa, wearing a low-cut sundress, and gazing up at him raptly. The only out-of-control fire in the room was the one blazing in her eyes.

Anger boiled up in him, but it was instantly drowned by a tidal wave of red-hot desire when she shifted her leg so that her skirt shimmied down to her thighs. "What are you doing here?"

She uncurled herself from the couch, picked up a bouquet of red roses, and sashayed over to him. She held out the overpowering scented roses to him. "I want to apologize again for my sister and Ian. I've been waiting for you for hours. I began to fear you weren't coming home tonight."

"I was at the gym, working out." He eyed the flowers, not sure what to do with them. A woman had never given him flowers before. It felt somehow backwards.

"You should put those in a vase with water." The vixen seemed able to read his mind and he scowled.

"Uh. Right." *Duh!* He stomped to the kitchen, found a crystal vase, and stuck the roses in it. He felt silly carrying them to the dining room like he was some beauty pageant contestant. *Did real men get roses?*

"So, you really didn't have a patient to visit tonight?" Wendy strolled over to him, and arranged the roses attractively. She brushed up against him, her breasts grazing his arm.

His temperature rocketed and his chest grew tight. He eyed her warily, trying not to let his gaze dip to danger zones such as those luscious breasts that were ready to spill out of her halter-top at the slightest movement. "I thought we established that earlier. Why all the candles?"

Tossing a sassy grin up at him, she plucked a rose from the bouquet. She twirled it in her fingers and then stroked the satiny petals down the column of his throat. With a wicked grin, she broke the stem and stuck it in her hair. "I thought they gave the place a little ambience. They cast a romantic glow, don't you think?"

His heart stopped. His tongue grew thick. "Are you trying to seduce me?"

She rubbed up against him, and slid her hands up his chest. Pressing herself against him, she clasped her arms about his neck. Her fingers played in the hair at the nape of his neck. She was on fire and her heat seeped into him. She raised her mouth to his and nibbled his lower lip playfully and wiggled against him erotically. "Um hm. Is it working?"

Desire slammed through him and he was extremely aware of those breasts pillowed against him. He wanted to feel them naked, massaging his bare chest.

Slowly, he untied her top and let the soft cotton slither down to her waist. "Perhaps."

She purred and arched closer to him, offering herself. Mischief danced in her eyes. "When will you know?"

Ashley Ladd

"Oh, maybe after I try a little taste of your nipples." A primitive growl rumbled in his stomach and his cock strained against her, demanding release.

"Feast away." She linked her fingers through his and led him to the couch. She stretched out on it seductively and crooked her finger for him to join her.

While he still retained a shred of sanity, he asked, "Are you sure you want me to do this?"

When she lifted her gaze to him, passion blazed in her eyes. "I'm on fire for you. I have been for a long time."

Surprise coursed through him. And delight. He lowered himself atop her, careful not to crush her with his weight, and buried his head between those too-tempting breasts, licking each nipple, pleased when they pebbled with her desire. "How long?" He'd only picked up on her signals for the past few weeks.

"Almost forever." She writhed against him, making him crazy.

He slid a hand beneath her skirt and found the source of her heat. Cupping her mound, he rubbed his thumb over her hardening clit. His breath caught in his throat when all he felt was bare, shaven skin. *No underwear. No curls. Had he really thought she was a goody-two-shoes? The wholesome girl-next-door?* "I think it's working," he said huskily. Raw need slammed through him and he wrestled the offending skirt up around her waist to give him better access to her treasures.

Her fingers tangled in his hair, caressing his scalp. When he dipped his finger in her well, she moaned. Her tight cunt sheathed him, fluttering deliciously. She was so hot and wet, so ready to be fucked. He sucked her hungrily, pulling as much of her generous breast into his mouth as he could.

"Take your clothes off. Fuck me," she pleaded, raw hunger in her voice.

He couldn't stop their coupling now anymore than he could stop an oncoming hurricane. Riptides threatened to suck him under and drown him in her spell. He hated to release her breast, but hoisted himself off her. Towering over her, he tore his shirt off and kicked his slacks across the room. His cock sprung out, crimson and pulsing, already slick with his need for her.

He wanted to savor their first time together, but he was ready to explode. Judging by her passion glazed eyes, so was she. He already knew she was well lubricated and ready for him.

With a growl, he thrust into her, careful at first so as not to hurt her. He had been told his length was quite impressive and many women couldn't take his full shaft.

She groaned and opened her legs wider, and wrapped one around him. Her writhing drove him mad, pushing him to greater heights, shoving him to the brink of ecstasy. Her cunt was deep and tight, gloving all of him. It milked him, squeezing him tightly.

He captured her lips and drank of her deeply. Their tongues mated wildly. Then, gasping for air, on the brink of climax, he mumbled against her lips, "We definitely should have done this earlier."

"Now that we have, I vote we never stop." She ground her pussy against him, bucking zealously.

Fire engine sirens broke through his passion and he swore. He'd forgotten to call them back and tell them it was a false alarm. "Shit!"

She raked his back with her nails, refusing to let him go. Then she screamed in ecstasy, as her vagina clenched him and shuddered lusciously.

A million stars exploding in his universe, his own release burst forth and he shot waves of seed into her. As much as he longed to hold and cuddle her, kiss her eyelids and suckle her breasts some more, he knew they were about to have company. Frustrated, he tugged her skirt down and tossed her top up. "Tie that, fast."

He snatched his shirt and went in search of his slacks that were God only knew where. Heavy footsteps clumped up the stairs, warning him time was up.

Banging rocked the door. "Fire department. Open up. You okay in there? We heard a woman scream. Someone called about a fire."

Wendy's face suffused deep burgundy as she grabbed up his slacks and threw them at him. "Catch," she hissed.

Hopping on one foot, he thrust his other leg into his slacks. Tripping, he pitched forward, but caught himself on the couch.

"We're fine!" Wendy yelled as she strode to the door with amazing grace under the circumstances and opened it.

A short, stocky middle-aged man with shoulder-length hair and a goatee peered inside. The hatchet in his hands was almost half his height. "Someone reported a fire at these premises?"

Trace swore under his breath as he wrenched his zipper up and stuffed his shirttails into his waistband. His knee sore where he had twisted it, he limped to the door and stood behind Wendy. "That was me. It turned out my girlfriend had lit all these candles and it looked like fire from outside." He gestured to the dancing flames visible through the dining room entryway.

The man took a couple steps inside and peered into the room. "You should have let us know."

Chagrined, Trace smiled apologetically and raked his fingers through his spiky hair a la Wendy. "I meant to, but uh, got distracted."

The fireman nodded. "What about the scream I just heard." He squinted at Wendy who was also finger combing her hair. "Are you okay, Miss?"

Her chest heaved and she sought Trace's hand and squeezed it. "I'm fine. We were uh…" She shrugged prettily and averted her still passion-darkened eyes.

Trace nodded at the man and shrugged also.

The fireman backed toward the door, looking embarrassed. "Oh, right. We're glad to hear everybody's okay. And miss," He shot a fatherly look at Wendy, "Next time you want to surprise your boyfriend with candlelight—tell him first."

Wendy shifted her weight from foot to foot and nodded. "I'm so sorry. It never occurred to me he'd think the house was on fire."

The man tipped his shiny hat to her. "Be sure you douse all those candles before you fall to sleep so we don't get called back for real."

Trace swallowed hard. "Will do." He shut the door securely behind the public servant and locked it. Then he turned to face Wendy, crossing his arms over his chest. With her face flushed and her hair mussed from his lovemaking, she stole his breath. He had never seen her looking so radiantly beautiful. Now, that he could think clearly, he remembered her earlier words. "I thought you wanted to talk to me about something important?"

She licked her lips and clasped her hands behind her. Secrets flittered across her amazingly piquant eyes. "I do." Her gaze flitted to the dining room. "Let's go sit down first."

He captured her hand in his, noticed how perfectly it fit, and laced his fingers through hers. Tugging gently, he led her to the dining room, sat in his favorite recliner and pulled her onto his lap. Not wanting her to escape, he wound his arms around her waist and buried his face in her flowery scented hair and inhaled deeply. "Okay, let's talk."

She squirmed and twisted around in his arms to face him. Her expression was almost as sober and scared as when she'd walked into her mother's hospital room a few weeks ago, alarming him. Inhaling deeply, she trembled. "You know Skye Blue..."

The rock star was a fragrant, but fading memory. Wendy must be jealous after all. Like he was of Mr. Hair. "Skye who?" Starved for another taste of her, he traced her tempting lips with the pad of his thumb, anxious for her to exorcise the dragon that troubled her.

Apprehension chased across her face instead of the relief he expected. A frown tugged at his lips. "You don't need to be jealous of her."

"I don't?" She almost sounded disappointed, so he gave into his desire and kissed her soundly as he let his hands massage her trim waist. He broke the kiss when her response was lukewarm.

Troubled himself now, he leaned his forehead against hers and peered into her eyes. "No. She was just an interlude. Not the real thing. I couldn't live with her lifestyle or fame, and I doubt she'd give up her career for someone like me—not that we were ever more than a one-night stand."

To his astonishment, Wendy pulled back further and the atmosphere cooled at least twenty degrees. Ice chilled her glare and froze her muscles. *What had he missed? Maybe she hadn't understood what he was trying to tell her.*

He tried again. "I don't love Skye Blue. I don't desire Skye Blue. She's not my type." There, that should be clear enough to erase her jealousy.

Wendy unclasped his hands from around her middle and stood up unsteadily. Shadows flickered across her pale, pinched face and she gazed at him sadly. "I need to make a confess…"

More banging rattled the door. "Trace! Trace! Come quickly! Mama's fallen and I think she's dying," Angel screamed frantically.

Adrenaline pumping through him, he jumped out of his chair, grabbed his medical bag from his car, and ran to Bessie's house.

* * * * *

Wendy reached her mother a few steps ahead of Trace. Her heart beating wildly, her chest aching, she gulped in a huge lungful of air. Fear cascaded through her and she knelt by her ashen-faced sister who cradled their mother in her arms.

Angel held her tenderly, rocking back and forth on her heels. "I told her not to do too much too soon. She wouldn't listen."

Wendy sought her mother's pulse and exhaled in relief when she found it beating vigorously, if rapidly. She stroked her mother's clammy hand, tracing the raised blue vein with her fingertip. She lifted her gaze to her sister's furrowed face. "What did she do?"

Trace knelt beside them, his presence comforting despite the fact he had confessed that he did not desire or want her. Or rather, it was his status as her mother's physician that leant a measure of comfort and strength, not the man himself, Wendy told herself. He took her mother in his arms and laid her flat on the floor, and then examined her.

Wendy's heart somersaulted in her chest as she waited his diagnosis with bated breath. "Will she be okay?"

Bessie's lashes fluttered weakly and her eyes opened to mere slits. "Why are you huddled around me? What happened?" Her voice was almost as weak as a kitten.

Angel grasped their mother's hand between both of hers and kissed it. "You collapsed, Mama. You tried to do too much, too soon. You frightened me to death. I thought we were going to lose you."

Wendy held her mother's other hand and squeezed it. "You're not Super Woman. None of us are. You're supposed to be taking it easy so you will regain your full strength."

Bessie gaped at her, color flooding back into her cheeks, and the twinkle sparkling in her eyes. "Why? So you can hurry up and desert me again?"

Guilt slammed into Wendy's chest and it took everything she had to keep her smile in place. "I'm not leaving." *Not yet. Not until she absolutely had to.*

Trace shot her a crushing, disbelieving glare.

He didn't believe her. He obviously considered her a vagabond, also.

Isn't that what she was? A vagabond? Traveling from one one-night-stand to the next? Never putting down roots in any town? Well, she did have a luxurious condo in L.A., but she was rarely permitted to enjoy it because of the band's hectic schedule. It looked more like an impersonal hotel than a real home.

"Let's get you into bed so you can get some of that rest the doctor ordered." When Bessie struggled to rise, Trace frowned, scooped her up, and carried her to her bed as if she was no heavier than an infant.

Angel twittered about Bessie's room, cackling, not giving their mother a moment's peace. Her eyes were feverish and her breathing was shallow.

Wendy bet that her sister's blood pressure was higher than their mother's, not that her own was exactly excellent at the moment either. Worry consumed her and she put an arm around Angel's shoulders. "You look tired. You need to get some rest, too."

Angel looked at her as if she'd sprouted two additional heads. "I can't leave, Mama. I'm going to sit with her in case she wakes up and needs anything."

Alarm jolted Wendy. "You won't be any good to Mom or yourself if you don't get your rest."

"Then we'll take shifts. I'll take the first." Angel shrugged away from her and stationed a chair at their mother's bedside and plopped into it. She leaned forward and laid her head on the mattress and gazed at the older woman.

"We both have commitments. Your pageant. My work. We'll call the nurse back."

* * * * *

Storm had an appearance scheduled in Key West two nights hence.

Angel lifted her head and nodded. She tried to stifle a yawn and failed. "It's too late to call her tonight. It's after one in the morning."

"To bed with you. A beauty queen needs her beauty rest. You don't want puffy eyes for the preliminaries, do you?" Wendy tried to pull her sister up. She was heartened by their mother's peaceful snoring and the steady rise and fall of her chest. *Now, to coax her sister into a similar restful state.*

Wendy was still wondering what had happened to her mother. "How did Mom fall?"

Angel sighed and tied her hair into a knot at the nape of her neck. "A siren woke her up and she couldn't get back to sleep. So, she went out to the kitchen to get herself a midnight snack, saw that the dishwasher had just finished, and she tried to put the dishes away herself. She fell off the step ladder when she was trying to reach the top shelf in the upper cabinet."

Wendy sucked in a huge gulp of air. It was her fault. The firemen had only come because she'd lit those lousy candles in her lame attempt to seduce Trace. Instead of being a night to remember fondly, it would be a black day in history. First, the debacle with Trace, and then her mother's mishap.

* * * * *

Monsters invaded her dreams that night, and Wendy awoke in a clammy sweat, her sheets and nightshirt soaked in her perspiration. She'd dreamed of disaster and disgrace. Never one to believe in premonitions, she tried to put it down to recent events. If the events of the past week progressed naturally, disaster to her personal life and career was eminent. *She had to tell Trace.*

She squinted at her digital alarm clock radio and groaned when it read seven A.M. In her profession, she didn't know what the world looked like at that time of day. Birds twittered outside her window and rays of sunlight tortured her eyes when she inched her aromatherapy night mask off her forehead.

The birds could stay. The bright light had to go. She rose to her knees, yanked her curtains tightly shut, and then scooted off her bed. Her comforter tangled around her ankles, tripping her and she fell backward onto the mattress. "Mornings are hell," she mumbled. Only masochists awoke early without a life and death reason. No wonder she'd given them up eons ago.

She fought off the covers and tossed them onto the bed. Then she padded to the shower and made herself human again with cucumber-melon gel she found hanging in the stall. It smelled heavenly and she inhaled greedily.

Still only half awake despite the refreshing water, she towel dried the excess water from her hair, combed it, and then slipped on culottes. Her eyes still ached and she slid her sunglasses onto her nose, held her hands before her and went in search of coffee.

"The mummy returns," Angel murmured dryly from her mother's bedroom door.

"Coffee," Wendy's raspy voice barely croaked out of her mouth. "Killer, black espresso. Full octane."

Angel trod after her and made a futile attempt to hide a wide yawn behind her hand. "If you want espresso, find a Cuban café."

Barbaric! What civilized person didn't own an espresso machine? Of course, she hadn't missed it till today when she needed an emergency dose. She tossed a glance full of pity at her sibling. She would have to buy an espresso machine for her deprived family.

"How did Mom rest?" Wendy took comfort in the fact that her easily panicked sister appeared calm, despite being grouchy.

"She slept through the night. I thought I'd fix a light breakfast for her before she awakes." Angel put two slices of bread in the toaster. "Do you want some?"

Wendy shook her head. Their mother's rich cooking was beginning to show on her hips. "Just coffee and grapefruit for me." She'd missed having a grapefruit tree in her backyard and enjoyed their homegrown specialty. She poured her coffee and sliced a grapefruit in half and savored it at the kitchen table.

Angel plucked another grapefruit from the bowl and joined her at the table, smoothing her robe beneath her. "Trace called and said he'd be out of town this weekend and to call Dr. Harper if Mom gets worse or needs anything."

Wendy's heart somersaulted. *Did that mean Trace would show up at the Key West concert? To see the woman whom he didn't love or desire?* She tried to drown her bitterness in a swig of coffee and burned her tongue. Served her right. Careful to sound nonchalant, she asked, "Did he say where he was going?"

Angel stirred creamer into her coffee and stared into the misty mocha whirlpool. "Probably to see Skye Blue, where else? Storm's in Key West this weekend."

"That close?" Trace would have a lot of nerve showing his face at another Storm concert. *Did he expect her to welcome him to her bed again?*

She scrunched her nose, speared a chunk of the juicy grapefruit, and ripped the meaty fruit apart with her teeth. Of course, he didn't know that he'd told Skye Blue that he didn't love or desire her, and that she was just a one-night stand. That should have made her Wendy half ecstatic, but her Skye Blue half seethed.

If he dared show up at another Storm concert, let him beware. He would not know what hit him.

* * * * *

"Something wrong, luv?" Thunder placed his fingers on the edges of Wendy's down turned lips and forced them up. "Is it that lesbian love nest thing?"

It hadn't been until he reminded her. "Thanks. I'd managed to forget about that for a few hours."

He brushed his glorious mane, looking like the king lion he was. "So, what's eating you?"

Bad choice of words. She was trying to forget about Trace and their previous encounters at Storm's Florida concerts. She snarled at him and pulled his hair.

Thunder jumped back and crossed his fingers at her. "Don't mess up the hair." He sprayed a fine mist of aerosol over it, then fluffed it with his fingers. Lascivious lights sparkled in his eyes. "You only get to touch it under one circumstance."

"Oh, puh-leaze. Give it a break." She couldn't handle one man between the two of her, much less two peculiar men.

Roger rushed in at his usual warp speed. "Oxygen! The press is smothering me out there." Emerald lightning flashed in the manager's eyes. "They all want an exclusive about your secret lovers. We've got to throw them a bone."

Mutinous, she thrust out her jaw and squared her shoulders. "I've not had a chance to tell my family yet."

Disbelief warred in her manager's eyes but his breathing eased. "So, tell them already!" He tossed his cell phone to her. "The call's on my dime. Tell them now so we can go on stage and clear this up."

Stingy Roger wouldn't offer to pay if he wasn't seriously upset. "I can't tell them over the phone. I have to do it in person."

Roger threw up his hands and cried, "Why me?" Then he glared at Thunder. "Make her listen to sense."

Thunder cocked his head and regarded Roger as if he were a specimen from another planet, and then broke out in hearty laughter. "Since when does she listen to me? I've been telling her to come clean for the past month and you can see how well I'm getting through."

"I was about to tell them when my mother had a relapse." That was at least ninety percent true. "If I tell her now, it'd be like pushing her into the grave." And dumping dirt on her casket.

Roger stepped into her private restroom and loosed a blood-curdling scream that should have brought the police down upon them if not for all the noise in the stadium. Then he slammed the door and marched over to her, his face cherry red. "You're pushing me into an early grave! Don't I count?"

She winced but steeled herself against his pompous tone. Melodramatic Roger had put on some Emmy award winning performances to get his way in the past. "I have to clear it with my mother's doctor."

Thunder swallowed his laughter and skipped out the door.

"Coward!" she yelled at his back, her fingers itching to strangle the deserter.

"So, call her doctor!" Roger's eye ticked rapidly as did the pulse at the base of his throat.

Acid reflux bubbled in her chest and she groaned. She did not need this right now. *How was she supposed to sing like a songbird when she was being made out to be a Benedict Arnold?* "What part of 'no' don't you understand? It could be detrimental to my mother's health."

Thunder stuck his head in the door carefully as if scared he would get a shoe in the face. "Time's up. The crowd is calling for us."

Chanting echoed in the huge coliseum. Then about a million feet stomped, shaking the foundation. "They really might bring down the house."

"What does it matter? You're killing us anyway."

She ignored Roger's monumental pout and swept past him regally. "People should learn to mind their own business."

"You're in the wrong business if you think there's a prayer of that." Thunder grasped her shoulders and followed her closely as if in a Conga line. His fingers massaged her tensed neck and she moaned.

"Why should anyone care who I sleep with? What does it matter?" She fumed and her veins bulged dangerously.

"I care, luv," Thunder murmured in her ear as he prodded her onstage. He scowled and pointed. "Your doctor friend's here again."

Disappointment and fury roiled in her gut. "He's not my friend."

Thunder shot her a look full of confusion. "Then why do you care if he knows or not? Why even bother to tell him. He can find out with the rest of your fans."

Conflicting emotions warred in her heart and she shrugged. "I don't know," she said contrarily, angrier at herself than at Trace.

Thunder shook his head and sighed. "You'd better decide before someone else decides for you. Trust me, it'll go down better if you come clean first." With that, he grabbed her hand and they ran onstage.

* * * * *

Trace hadn't planned to attend another Storm concert, but he'd been compelled. He couldn't stay away. His mouth watered when he spied the rock singer. The golden girl shimmered more radiantly than the sun. She eclipsed the moon and the heavens. Her golden voice could charm any man past puberty. Maybe they had a chance. Stranger things had happened.

And maybe he was Prince Charming. Right.

He was obviously psycho.

His heart palpitated when Skye's creamy jade gaze slithered over him and then looked quickly away as if he was beneath her contempt. Surely he had misread their expression. She couldn't hold the press attention against him, could she? The adverse publicity affected him more than her as no one knew her true identity. *Unless she was having an affair with the long-haired guitarist.*

He was used to being noticed, especially by her. Why the sudden arctic chill? *Almost as frozen as Freddie's icy glare.*

He evaluated the long-haired blond guitarist with narrowed eyes. *That blond hair couldn't be real, could it?* The band members probably all wore wigs, just as they painted their faces. Underneath their disguises, they were probably bald, or styled their hair in some preppy fashion.

He'd only ever seen authentic long, golden hair like that on one other man. Ian Keith, Freddie's ex-fiancé…

It couldn't be. Trace's heart stopped beating and he couldn't breathe.

Freddie's ebony hair could be as long as Skye Blue's shiny midnight blue tresses, if she ever let it down instead of tying it back in schoolgirl scrunchies…

He halted his ludicrous thoughts. Was he seriously imagining for a second that Wendy Applegate could be Skye Blue? He couldn't imagine anyone less likely.

But Freddie had been away a long time. Both women stood about the same height and build. They shared the same hair color. Freddie had disappeared every weekend since her homecoming. She was no longer a little mouse. She had liked to sing as a kid. And he had walked in on her coaching her sister in the art of singing…

He stared at the vision in black, trying to superimpose Freddie's features on the painted ones of Skye Blue. Creamy jade eyes flashed liquid fire at him. Freddie had blue eyes, the shade of the deepest ocean depths.

Relief slammed into his chest and he released a pent-up sigh. He felt silly, thinking the girl-next-door could have grown up to be a world-renowned rock star. Foolish dreams had no place in reality. It wasn't as if the world had a short supply of diminutive dark-haired women. They ran rampant in South Florida.

* * * * *

Wendy began coughing halfway through the set. Hoarse by the time the concert was over, her raw throat ached. She shivered despite the perspiration trickling between her breasts. It was all she could manage to hold her pounding head up and get herself offstage erect.

Thunder schlepped offstage behind her, his hair drenched. "Your voice was off tonight, Skye."

A coughing fit wracked her body. "I'm not feeling well." The room spun dizzily and she slumped to the floor as everything went dark.

She awoke in her dressing room, prone, covered with scratchy blankets. Several people huddled over her, worried creases marring their foreheads. Concern pooled in their eyes.

"Whath hap-hened?" Thick and grainy, her tongue made speech difficult. Fog clouded her mind and she had trouble thinking clearly.

"Your doctor friend was waiting for you, so we enlisted his aid," Roger said, squeezing her hand. Hovering beside her, a worried frown creased his forehead.

"You collapsed. You're running a high fever," Trace said, stepping into her field of vision. "How long have you been feeling ill?"

Her eyes wide, she croaked, "It started this morning." Luckily, the coarse voice that tumbled off her lips didn't sound like her own. She didn't want him to learn her true identity this way. *If he didn't know already...* Her fingers flew to her face to see if her paint was intact and was relieved to feel the greasiness.

"What's wrong with her?" Thunder asked. "It's not pneumonia is it?"

"We'll have to run some tests. It's probably just a flu..." Trace grasped her wrist and felt for her pulse. His fingers were warm and gentle on her flesh.

She writhed and yelled, "No! I want my doctor." Her voice still hoarse, came out in a froggy stage whisper, unidentifiable as feminine much less her own voice.

Pain flickered across Trace's eyes before the shutters fell. His face a mask, he lowered her arm to the table, and then stepped back. To Roger who had stepped forward as her spokesperson, Trace said, "As the patient wishes. But I would bring him in immediately. We don't know what we're dealing with."

Then Trace looked at her, his expression inscrutable. "I won't be overstepping any more bounds." With that, he pivoted on his boot heel and strode away.

Thunder eyed her speculatively, but waited to speak until the door had closed behind Trace. He clucked his tongue and shook his head. "Not good, luv."

Roger's face was flushed and feral eyes glowed above his pudgy cheeks. Blustery, he heaved a huge sigh and glowered down at her. "Don't start going diva on us. What was wrong with that doctor?"

Thunder removed the makeup from her face gently.

"It's personal," she mumbled.

Roger threw up his hands and moaned aloud. He turned to Thunder. "Can you tell me what's going on?"

Wendy pulled Thunder's finger to get his attention. "Not if he wants to live."

Thunder shrugged at their manager and in his best Sergeant Schultz imitation, he said, "I know nothing!"

Roger flipped open his cell phone and stabbed in a number, then spoke heatedly into the receiver. "The doctor has a colleague meeting us at the local hospital."

Another coughing attack sent her into worse spasms than the last. She doubled over, holding her stomach. Her throat felt like it was being ripped from her body.

Roger ambled over and stroked damp hair out of her face. "You poor dear. Sorry I had a snit fit. I just worry about my favorite people." He put his arm around her shoulders and helped her sit up. "Think you can walk to the car? You can lean on me."

Thunder grimaced and scooped Wendy into his arms. "She can barely breathe. Let's go. Wrap another blanket around her."

Roger swaddled her like a baby, and opened the door for them to pass thru.

A camera flashed in her eyes, blinding her. Instinctively, she turned her face into Thunder's chest.

"Gotcha!" A lizardlike smile curled the man's lips as he slithered into the shadows.

"Damn!" Roger echoed her thoughts aloud.

"It was bound to happen," Thunder said, resignation ringing in his voice.

Wendy groaned and lost consciousness.

Chapter Eleven

After two weeks at home in bed fighting pneumonia, feeling guilty about missing important concerts, Wendy was bone weary and strung out. The worst and best parts were having Trace hover over her, the competent, caring caregiver.

The worst because the lies were wearing her out and to what point anyway? Surely Trace was starting to figure things out. He wasn't an idiot. Hell, maybe he had figured her out and was just baiting her for his own nefarious purposes. Wendy traced her suddenly dry lips with her tongue and wished her throat wasn't so very raw. Her time was running out if it hadn't already. "Close the door and lock it, please."

Mischief danced across his eyes as he did her bidding. "You're not up to…"

Frissons of awareness arced through her, much to her chagrin. She was too ill to do anything about it even if he didn't hate her after her revelations. Scowling at him, she patted the bed beside her for him to sit down. "There's something I need to tell you …privately."

Trace arched a brow and swaggered over to her, his demeanor changing subtly. He hooked his thumbs through his belt loops and towered over her instead of putting her at ease by sitting at a more comfortable eye-level. "You've been wanting to tell me something. What is it?"

She couldn't do this. She had to do this or someone else would do it for her and then heaven help her. She swallowed hard, and tried to muster up her courage. "I don't sell hygiene products. I don't sell anything." *Well, that sounded extremely articulate.*

Trace cocked his head to the side as if indulging her. "You don't help your fiancé sell condoms?"

This was difficult enough without snide comments. "I don't sell anything." Well, strictly speaking, she did earn her living selling her music…

"You're really engaged to Mr. Hair."

Frustrated by his interruptions and assumptions, she ground her teeth and glared up at him. "I'm not engaged to anyone." He wasn't making this easy. She wanted to scream!

"Why the big chill the other night?" His brows pinched together and his gaze dueled with hers.

Finally, the perfect moment to confess her dual identity! She inhaled deeply, and started coughing. She couldn't stop. She could barely breathe.

Trace gave her a glass of water. "Sip this." Then he sprung from the bed and gave her a shot of Albuterol so she could breathe. "Do you have a breathing machine?"

When she tried to answer, he held up his hand, stopping her. "Just nod. Don't try to talk."

Alarm flooded her as she heard the death knell tolling for her career. Never before had she needed a breathing machine. She prayed this bout with pneumonia wouldn't saddle her with asthma.

Sipping the water gingerly, the cool soothing liquid slid down her throat. Her wheezing slowly subsided, but her chest still felt as if an elephant lounged on it.

She shook her head, determined to confess the whole sordid truth. "I'm really…"

Trace put two fingers to her lips gently, sending shock waves down her spine. "Shush. Get some rest."

She couldn't afford to wait again. She was on borrowed time as it was. "But…"

He pierced her with a stern glare and folded his arms over his chest. "Doctor's orders," he said in a tone that brooked no argument. "Pneumonia isn't something to fool around with. Get some rest." He pivoted on his heel and ambled out of the room.

Great! She scooted down on the bed so that she lay prone, then stared at the ceiling. Maybe she should just send him an email. That seemed the only way to get her message to him. *With her luck, he'd probably think it was spam and delete it unread.*

* * * * *

Damn! He'd been waiting for her to come clean about whatever it was eating at her, and the truth had almost literally choked her. What deep dark secret was so very important she burned to tell him this minute?

That she was secretly engaged to Mr. Hair?

She was hiding a husband and kids somewhere?

She was going to have a sex change?

Or she was really Skye Blue in disguise?

Blinking at the most ridiculous thought he'd ever entertained, he awoke from his stupor. *Shy, self-effacing little Freddie was Skye Blue? What a joke.*

Or was it? Goose flesh rose on his arms as he stared off into space, his eyes narrowing. Freddie had long, ebony hair like Skye Blue's. Both women were about the same height and shape. And both of them were ill and bedridden at the same time with a similar ailment.

They couldn't be one and the same...could they?

Frowning, he shook himself. *Most certainly not.* Their eyes were different colors, they had different voices, and most important piece of evidence was that they had entirely opposing demeanors. He just had a bad case of Skye Blue on the brain. He couldn't get the sexy singer out of his mind, or the mystery about her secret identity.

His head pounding, he massaged his aching temples in a futile attempt to restore his shaky equilibrium. His thoughts spun dizzily, about as innocent as pure sin.

Crazy thinking! It was just wishful thinking that he had discovered Skye Blue's secret identity. Freddie was no more Skye Blue than she was Arnold Schwarzenegger.

* * * * *

I really should have sent that email. She was afraid she had squandered all her chances.

Sandwiched between her mother and Trace, Wendy chafed in her seat at the Miss Florida Pageant. Awaiting the judges' final decision was torture, plain and simple. If they didn't come back with a decision soon, her fingernails would be completely shredded and she'd pass out from holding her breath.

Not that she had much breath to hold. She'd barely recovered from her pneumonia, but couldn't miss the most important event of her sister's life. Her poor nerves were stretched taut, ready to break. She'd not seen or spoken to Trace in over two weeks since she'd been bedridden as he'd been called out of town on an emergency.

She couldn't confess her deepest, darkest secret through email. Nor over the phone. That was the coward's way out, and much too impersonal. But when could she tell him? Something or someone always interrupted.

Her mother squeezed her hand so tightly, the bones in her fingers ached. "She'll be crushed if she loses. She's waited for this her entire life."

"So have you," Wendy whispered back.

"What mother doesn't want her children to succeed?" Bessie turned her liquid silver eyes on her. "It's time for you to follow your dream. Make something more of yourself. Take a cue from your little sister."

Pinpricks of pain pierced her skull as they did every time she was compared to her sister and found wanting. Anxious to exonerate herself, but knowing this wasn't the time, she pursed her lips. She hoped her mother wouldn't call in a priest to exorcise the demons when she learned her eldest child was the scandalous Skye Blue.

Angel and the other four finalists held hands, as if in community prayer. Radiant smiles lit their exquisite faces. Light twinkled off their beautiful evening gowns. Tension shimmered in the air.

Wendy squeezed her mother's hand, her earlier observation forgiven. Trace laced his fingers through hers, and his warm hand rested on her knees, sending frissons of awareness up her leg. She tried not to quiver, but his touch set off wildfires. She had been on a Trace diet too long, and her starved body craved him.

Trace leaned over and whispered in her ear, his warm breath setting off her fire alarms. "What was it you wanted to tell me?"

Surprised, she recoiled and stared at him. Here? Now? Next to her mother? He had the lousiest timing imaginable. "Later," she hissed.

'World peace' time had arrived for the five lucky finalists.

The Emcee escorted Miss Keys to the question chair proudly, then he ripped open the envelope with her special question. The smile never leaving his face, he asked, "What is your dream for the future?"

The young woman's smile brightened as if she'd just won the lottery, and she crooned into her mike, "Thank you, Richard. My dream is to help the poor children of the world. After I complete my degree in pediatrics, I plan to volunteer a few years for the Peace Corps. The children are our future and it can't be healthy and happy unless they are. Only then can we achieve world peace."

The crowd roared its approval. Trace clapped perfunctorily and whispered in her ear, "Damn! That's a tough answer to beat. That world peace stuff gets them every time."

Oh, yeah. Wendy's thoughts turned to Nikolai and she shuddered. *Not that she didn't want world peace.*

"You don't want world peace?" Trace asked, looking at her as if she was a warmonger. He couldn't be expected to know what she was reading.

Okay, so Trace didn't read the same things she did. She'd have to lend him her books. He used to like horror and sci-fi, but she didn't know what he liked now that he was an adult.

The little Italian emcee puffed out his chest proudly as he escorted the taller Miss Jacksonville to the podium next. The svelte silvery-haired blonde contestant glistened like a million twinkling stars. Silky hair brushed against her creamy shoulders as she floated across stage in her wispy gossamer gown.

Richard wiped his brow with a handkerchief he pulled from his vest pocket, and then he opened the sealed envelope. "Are you ready?"

"I'm always ready for you, Dick darling," Miss Jacksonville crooned in her sultry Southern drawl.

Dick Darling stumbled over his tongue. "Wh-what have you done to make the bedroo- world a better place?"

Trace snickered and whispered in her ear, "Old Dick can't cut it anymore."

Wendy swallowed a smile. "And you could do better? Pretty faces don't affect you like that?"

Trace scowled at her. "I don't go in for all that glitz and glamour."

She couldn't resist taunting him. "What about Skye Blue? If she's not glitzy..."

Trace peered off into the distance and paused as if measuring his words. "Her voice attracted me. It's so...soulful...seductive..."

"Sinful..." Wendy added, mesmerized by his vision of her. Forgiveness crept into her heart.

"The bad girl that sings like a nightingale."

Maybe she should use that as her new logo. She tried to erase the moony smile off her face before he deduced the reason for it.

"So, you like bad girls?" She tingled all over, longing to be very bad, ultra-mega bad. When was this damned thing going to end? She vowed to confess the truth to him soon as she could get him in private.

"Love them." He eyed her speculatively. "Does that frighten you?"

She longed to show him how very much his comment titillated her. It was all she could do not to squirm in her seat and she was surprised she didn't spontaneously combust. She licked her feverish lips, and warned her tongue to behave. She leaned close to him and bathed his ear with her tongue, and then nipped the lobe. "How do you see me?"

He shuddered against her, delighting her. Then he stroked his chin as he regarded her closely. "You? You confuse me."

She pulled away a few inches so he could see her face and she batted her lashes at him. "How?"

"You were always the girl-next-door."

Her wicked smile came out to play. "Not in years," she purred. "If you think I'm still Miss-goody-two-shoes, think again." She could put an end to that thought real fast.

"It's difficult to change the image you've held of someone so long." He eyed her as if he expected her to admit she was Wonder Woman or one of the X-Men.

She curled her fingers around his, and murmured against his ear, "I need to tell you something. Outside."

Her mother elbowed her in the ribs. "Shush! Your sister's up. Front and center."

Wendy wanted to scream! Of course she wanted to hear her sister's answer and watch her win the crown, but she was constantly being interrupted. "Later," she whispered to Trace and tried to pull her hand from his grasp.

He tightened his fingers, keeping hers captive. He dragged their entwined hands to his lap and clamped his other hand over their united ones. His thumb caressed her knuckles, making rational thought impossible.

Beaming at the audience, Angel placed her hand on Richard's extended arm, and glided to the chair. Twinkles glittered in her hair as she stepped up to her seat.

"Here is your question, my dear." Richard gazed at Wendy's sister with adoration. "What do you believe is the one thing threatening our society more than any other, and what would you do to change it?"

Angel fixed her eyes on their mother. "I believe that the number one ailment our society, indeed our world suffers from, is that we have strayed from traditional family values. To combat this and turn our society around, we need to ban immoral behavior.

Parents, teachers, and community leaders should shun all entertainment and entertainers that would disembowel the family unit. For instance, we should boycott Storm concerts as Skye Blue is the anathema of all that is good in our society."

Wendy's heart shriveled and fell to her stomach. Her jaw dropped. *How could her own sister deliver such a death blow to her?*

A hush fell over the hall, and then Angel added quickly, "And of course, that will bring world peace."

Thunderous applause rocked the building, jolting Wendy out of her stupor. She wished it hadn't for she was going to be ill.

The lights dimmed for intermission while the judges cast their votes and decided which blessed contestant they would send on to compete for the crown of Miss USA. The excitement and mortification were too much for Wendy. She couldn't take anymore. Jumping up from her seat, she mumbled, "Excuse me," and crawled over her mother to escape.

"Wenefred! You can't leave now, when your sister's about to be crowned!" Bessie sounded appalled as she grabbed at Wendy's hand.

"I need some air." She began to hyperventilate, feeling like the unloved, forgotten little girl who was invisible to her parents. She had to escape before she thoroughly embarrassed herself.

"Wendy!" Trace swore under his breath and followed her. He caught up to her in the lobby, his iron hand clamping around her wrist. "What's going on? You're acting as if the devil's on your tail."

Wendy was about to hyperventilate, and pulled Trace off to the side. "You know how I've been trying to tell you something important?"

Trace's eyes darkened. "It's something to do with Ian Keith, isn't it?"

Not exactly. "He is involved, but it's not about him per se." Great! Now, he had the wrong impression.

"Are you in love with him? Is he leaving his wife for you?" Trace's hands fisted into white-knuckled balls. "What kind of game are you playing with me?"

Camera lights blinded her, and she held her hand up to ward off the paparazzi. *Oh, God. They'd found her.* She tried to sink into the wall and prayed it was only Trace they wanted to photograph. Then she remembered they'd caught her face without makeup on film before, too.

"What do you have to say for yourself, Skye Blue? I bet you didn't like what Little Sister had to say about you back there?" Slimy journalists pushed microphones at her and backed her against the wall.

"You've got the wrong woman," Trace said, snarling. "She's not Skye Blue."

"Wenefred Applegate aka Skye Blue," the reporter said with glee. "We finally figured out your secret identity."

Trace recoiled, staring at Wendy as if she'd sprouted horns. "You played me for a fool. I hope it was fun." He stormed off, his boot heels resounding like gunshots on the hard tile floor.

"Trace! Wait! Let me explain." Wendy tried to push past the suffocating journalists to no avail. They pinned her in the corner.

Guards marched over to them. "Break this up. The pageant's resuming."

"Yeah! Well, the big news is out here," a riled reporter shouted. "Skye Blue has been unmasked, and at her sister's pageant."

Other reporters from inside the hall poured into the lobby in a free-for-all.

"Ian Keith? Thunder?" A particularly pesky, shaggy-haired reporter wearing a ratty old fatigue jacket crowded her.

"Thunder?" Trace turned and stormed back, menace booming in his voice, anger flashing in his eyes. "I knew something was wrong with him. He's so hot for a threesome, why not you, he, and his wife? But leave me out of it." He pushed through the mob and strode away.

Shit! "That was his idea. I threw a shoe at him, remember?" But Trace had already turned his back on her and stalked off.

"…and Miss Tallahassee, Miss Brittany Otters, is our first runner up. In the event our new Miss Florida is unable to perform her duties, Brittany will step up and take the crown."

Happy squeals and catcalls assaulted Wendy's ears and she winced. "I really need to be in there with my sister." Wendy elbowed her way through the ocean of news people blocking her path.

"Which means that our new Miss Florida is Angelina Applegate!"

Wendy didn't get far. The commotion surrounding her drowned out the ceremony inside.

Trace stood sentinel at the doors, glaring at her. "You can't go in there and upstage her big night."

Wendy's stomach turned over and she gritted her teeth. "I'm not trying to upstage anyone. I just want to applaud my sister. Since when is that a sin?"

Disbelief contorted Trace's handsome features. "Since you lied to all of us."

The hair on the back of her neck bristled. People in glass houses… Of all the nerve. "Go ahead. Cast your stones. But you lied to me, too."

His eyes narrowed. "I never lied to you."

She struck a skeptical pose. "Oh yeah?"

"You told me you were through with Skye Blue. That your infatuation with her was history. Yet there you were, sniffing around her at her next concert in your leather gigolo outfit."

"You're talking about yourself in the third person." His clinical physician's tone irked her.

"You know what I mean." Her palms itched and she rubbed them down her dress.

Trace got up in her face, his breath scorching her flesh. "Lady. I don't have a clue what you're about or who you are, and I don't care to know."

The verbal slap stung more than any physical one ever could. "Fine! Then stop following me around."

"Don't come in my house uninvited."

"I'd rather visit a rattlesnake's nest."

A scrappy bright-eyed reporter interrupted, pointing at Trace. "Are you the dude in leather whose been seen at all her recent concerts? How do you spell your name?"

Murder flared in Trace's eyes. He snatched the notepad from him and shredded the paper.

The pup scout inched back, eying him warily.

"Go in with Angel. I know you're dying to."

"That's why I'm here." Trace pivoted on his heel and marched to her sister. He swung her into his arms, bent her back, and kissed her hard on the lips.

Wendy's heart shattered and she turned away, unable to watch. As usual, she was the outsider looking in, more than ever before. She wasn't welcome.

The reporters trailed her, blasting unrelenting questions at her which didn't register.

Suffocating, the toxic air pressed in on her, crushing her. She couldn't stay here, but she was trapped.

"There you are, luv," Thunder's lifesaving voice broke through her fog. He shoved his way into the inner circle.

Hugging her, stroking her hair, he didn't seem to notice or care about the barrage of cameras flashing in his face. "I'm here now. Everything will be okay."

Shell-shocked, she stared at the war zone. "It's just like you warned. Only worse."

"It always is. Come on. Let's get you out of here." Thunder parted the crowd, ignoring their impertinent questions, shielding her.

"You're really quite ordinary without your stage makeup, Skye. Some would say downright homely."

Wendy froze, drowning in pain.

Growling, Thunder drew her closer against him. "You'd best apologize to the lady."

"I s'pose that's why you hid your face under all that paint?"

"Yeah, too bad you're not beautiful like your sister. Maybe you should use some of your fortune to buy a new face."

She gasped.

Thunder snarled. "Leave her alone."

The press loved this massacre. Wendy tried to pull Thunder back. "We're just egging them on. Let Celia do all our talking."

A reporter with a death wish thrust a microphone in Thunder's face. "Is it true you're divorcing your hottie of a wife for this sow?"

Wendy flinched and vowed to get plastic surgery or move into a monastery.

Thunder tensed. "I warned you and now you've gone too far." He wrenched away from her and dove on the man, his fists flailing.

It took three burly security guards to tear them apart. Then they escorted them to a VIP vehicle and whisked them to safety.

"You're going home with us." Thunder flopped against the back seat and dragged in several huge gulps of air.

She inhaled sharply and touched his swelling bruises. "You're hurt."

"I couldn't stand by and let them say such things about you." He cracked half a grin and then winced.

"You silly man. What will your wife say?" Even Eskimos would hear this news.

A sigh shuddered through him and he shoveled unsteady fingers through his golden tresses. "She's already filed for divorce."

Regret assaulted her. "Why?"

"I told her I didn't love her. She freaked. Started throwing dishes at me. I left before she got to the knives."

And what did he expect? "I'm so sorry. We're a sad pair, aren't we?"

He cupped her face and caressed her lips with his. "I think we'd make a happy pair." He gazed deeply into her eyes, hope blazing.

Pity welled in her heart. She stroked his beloved face. If she had been blessed with a brother, she'd have chosen him. "I love you…but not that way."

"I'm a patient man. I know I blew it before. We'll take it slow." He sat forward and instructed the driver, "Please take us to Mermaid Grove."

She drew in a shuddering breath, mustering her courage. "No. I have to go home and face the music."

"It can wait till tomorrow."

"No. I have to do it now."

"They're probably celebrating and don't know your news yet. Don't spoil their night."

If she didn't do it now, she might never find the courage again. She shook her head. "It can't wait."

"Then I'm going with you." He gave the driver her address.

Her mother's yard looked like a zoo. News vans and cars littered the lawn. Reporters and photographers laid in wait.

"Turn around," Thunder ordered.

"Don't."

"This is insanity! They'll eat us alive."

"Get me close to the door." She scrunched up her face. "Please wait for me." She slipped the driver two crisp one hundred dollar bills.

The uniformed guard nodded and pulled up to the steps.

"You're nuts!" Thunder shook his head

"So, what's new? I'm still not as crazy as you."

Thunder cracked a grin. "That's not saying much. Let's get this over with. I'll go first. Stay right behind me."

She gathered what wits she had left. "Get ready. One. Two. Three. Go!"

It was like swimming upstream in a school of piranha. She held onto Thunder tightly and buried her face against his back.

Finally, they made their way inside.

Her mother and sister glared at her as if she was a criminal. A firing squad would look friendlier.

Bloodshot eyes and tear-blurred makeup ravaged Angel's face. Her sister trembled. "How could you ruin the biggest day of my life?"

Wendy recoiled. "I didn't want that to happen. I had no idea it would."

"You knew you were Skye Blue and that the paparazzi was closing in on you." Bessie fixed her with a quelling look.

True. Guilt wracked Wendy, scraping her nerves. "I was going to tell you right after the pageant. I didn't want to ruin your big moment."

"Why didn't you tell us before? You've been leading this double life for years. Don't you think we had a right to know?" Pain pinched her mother's mouth and she lowered herself into her favorite lounger.

Wendy dropped her gaze. "I was afraid you'd react like this. I've never been good enough for you. I was never pretty enough, talented enough, or smart enough for you and Daddy." She looked up at her mother. "I had to prove to myself I wasn't worthless, that I was somebody. But I never meant to hurt you." Or Trace. She wrung her hands together and looked heavenward for inspiration. "I was wrong. Please accept my apologies."

"I waited and worked for this day my entire life. And my big sister stole it from me." Angel gazed upon her newly won crown with disdain, as if the sight of it sickened her. A sneer twisted her lovely features. "You have the spotlight all the time. Everyone knows your name. You're rich and famous. Are you so jealous of me that you have to ruin my big moment?"

Sharp pain stabbed Wendy. She had never been in the spotlight at home with their parents. Angel had always taken the spotlight. Angel had been their parents' adored one, the one who received all their attention, the one on whom they pinned all their hopes and dreams. How could she have the spotlight when she'd been invisible? She stepped forward and reached out, only to have her heart torn from her when her sister flinched. "I swear I had no idea that would happen. I thought I had more time…"

"You knew it could happen?" Angel, now greener than her dress, looked as if she wanted to spit on her. "And you didn't warn us? You left it until my pageant. You make me sick! I can't even look at you." With that, Angel sobbed, ran out of the room, and slammed a door.

Her mother stared at her with watery eyes and closed the distance between them. They stared at each other several seconds, and then Bessie pulled her into a hug. "How could you ever think I don't love you? And if your father or I made you feel second best, I'm sorry. You're too self-effacing. Stop hiding all your talent beneath that hideous mask."

*Hideous…*So, she should bring her homely face out of the closet? She sucked in her breath. Her heart fell to her feet. The choice had been ripped from her. Pictures of her sans costume would surely be plastered all over the scandal sheets by morning. She bet her popularity took a nose-dive. Too many people equated physical beauty with worth.

"So, you forgive me?" Wendy pulled back enough to study the flickering emotions shadowing her mother's face.

Bessie converted to true form and snorted. "I'm working on it. I wish you had given us the benefit of the doubt." She turned her gaze on Thunder who awaited patiently, his hands linked behind his back. "And you, young man, did you tell your family about your career and dual identity?"

Thunder cleared his throat and shifted his feet. "Yes, ma'am. They've known from the beginning."

Bessie grimaced and made the sign of the cross over her chest. "And you didn't advise my girl to tell her own mama?"

Thunder looked uncomfortable but stilled his tongue. He cast Wendy a stern glance.

Wendy stepped forward. "He advised me to tell you many times. It's not his fault."

"Well, you've always been hard-headed. I guess that's been an asset in your career." Her mother peered closely at her. "Just how filthy rich are you? Haven't your records gone platinum?"

Wendy wasn't comfortable discussing money. "I do okay, Mom."

"She'll never have to worry about her finances." Thunder gazed at her proudly.

No. She only had to worry about her love life and familial relationships.

"Are you...?" Bessie watched her intently.

Wendy regarded her mother quizzically, longing to pull the words from her mouth.

"Are you a lesbian?"

"How could you ever think that?"

"I can vouch she's not," Thunder said in a low rumble.

A sharp intake of breath from the kitchen area startled Wendy. She glanced over to catch Trace lounging against the doorframe. His arms were folded across his chest, his eyes dark glittering pools.

Wendy turned and punched Thunder in the shoulder, and gave him a quelling look. "Stop that."

"And so what is your relationship with my daughter?" Bessie lifted her chin regally and pinned him in her sights.

Trace pushed off the wall with his foot and he stepped out of the shadow. Danger flared in his eyes. "He's married."

Wendy's heart screeched to a stop. Had he been there the entire time, skulking in the shadows? Waiting to pounce on her?

Purple rage suffused her mother's face. Her body shook visibly and the blue veins on the top of her hands bulged. "Married! I didn't bring you up to consort with married men, young lady. Where there's smoke, there's fire. Maybe you are as wild as those muck rags make you out to be?"

Not even half...not even a quarter as wild as her mother thought her. She led a downright mundane existence. Her usual daily routine resembled that of her mother's China dolls that peered at her sightlessly from their glass encased curio cabinet. Her shoulders sagged but only half as far as her spirits. "You know me. I'm not like that."

Trace smirked and his brow tented. Indignation rolled off him.

Bessie sniffed and dabbed her eyes with her tissue. "If you'll excuse me, I'm going to hit the sack. I'm just plumb worn out from all this upset."

Thunder regarded her with sympathy.

Trace dropped a hand to her mother's shoulder and squeezed it comfortingly. "You'd better get some rest. It's been a trying day. You don't want to have a relapse."

"I suppose you're going off with your married lover?" Bessie blew her nose and then pocketed the tissue in her robe. "Now I see where you were running off to constantly." With that, her mother sighed heavily and ambled to her room.

"I think you'd better leave now. They need some peace and rest." Trace towered over her, his shadow falling ominously across hers.

Wendy bristled. Pain slashed her with hurricane force. *She wasn't welcome in her own home?* "Leave? You mean as in don't sleep here? Don't come back?"

Trace nodded and stood stoic. After several tense moments, he said, "It'd be best for everyone if you give them some time to get used to the idea."

"And what about you?" She craned her neck to gaze up at him. "You need time to sort things out, too?"

"There's nothing to sort out. You played me for a fool. You didn't trust any of us. You're in a relationship with a married man." He swaggered to the door and rattled the knob. "It's late."

Much too late. She faced off against him, her hands on her hips, her toes curling inside her shoes. "I've told you till I'm blue in the face that Ian and I are just friends. Why won't you believe me?"

Trace scowled. "You disguised yourself and lured me into your bed under false pretenses. You didn't let me know who you really were."

"As I recall," she pushed the distracting wisps of hair off her forehead and tucked them behind her ears, "you came on to me."

"Practically stalked her, old man," Thunder cut in.

"I didn't know who you really were." Trace's nostrils flared.

Logic didn't flow from his premise and she frowned. "Of course you didn't know Skye Blue's identity. As far as anyone knew, she could be anyone, even the girl-next-door." The gears in her mind ground loudly. "But what you're really saying is that you expected Skye Blue to be beautiful, and glittery, and sexy, out of disguise." *Not some ogre.*

He snarled, his forehead creasing. "Don't go putting words in my mouth. You should have been up front with me."

Thunder's gaze glowed softly over her, but grew harsh when it swiveled on Trace. "Grab your stuff and stay with the band until we can leave this alligator infested swamp."

Trace guarded the door as she cleaned out her room and wished it a silent goodbye. It wasn't her anymore: the pink lacy frills, the cute knick-knacks, and the eyelet comforter.

She was a woman now who no longer liked lacy frills. She went for sexy red satin and black leather… It was time to put the past behind her, starting with the hostile, obdurate doctor. No longer would she care what others thought of her, especially him. Everything of any value to her fit in her one piece of luggage which she wheeled behind her.

"Maybe if you'd let me explain…listen…"

Trace snorted. "I can't listen to unspoken words. You had plenty of opportunity to come clean...and didn't." He opened the door and strode out. His fierce expression kept the mob at bay. Not surprising, the feral light in his eyes would ward off a multitude of monsters.

Thunder shrugged. "His loss." When they ventured outside, he gazed up at the night sky. "Yep. It's a full moon all right."

"I guess it's true that all the crazies come out." Not only was it a full moon, but blood rimmed it. *Eerie.* Chills crept up her spine.

Thunder herded her to the car, fending off the paparazzi. "Don't tell me you believe in the boogie man and monsters under the bed? You're much too grounded for all that new age paranormal bullshit."

Really? Then she wouldn't admit she'd had childhood nightmares about swamp monsters with huge crocodile heads that crawled out of the canal behind their house specifically to haunt her. Of course, they looked friendly in comparison to this swarm and in particular compared to Trace.

Her glance strayed to Trace's house. It was pitch black and his car was nowhere in sight. "Get me out of here."

Thunder opened the car door for her and then loaded her bag in the trunk. Then he slipped onto the seat beside her and slammed the door.

He sat forward. "You may want to call for police escort, chap. I don't fancy us being run into a canal by our friends." He scowled at a reporter who pressed his nose against the car window.

The hired security nodded and called for escort.

Once they were moving safely, Wendy slipped off her shoes and wriggled her toes. "You know this means we can't ever enjoy a normal life again." She lamented being inconspicuous, of going wherever she chose to, whenever she wanted.

Thunder patted her hand. "Back home in L.A., no one'll bother you. I can't wait to get out of this bayou and back to civilization."

She couldn't wait to see this town in the rear view mirror, either.

Chapter Twelve

What lousy dimension had he slid into?

Night was day. Day was night. Long held conceptions were wrecked to hell. Sweet, innocent girls-next-door were really changelings; dangerous, deadly creatures, completely illogical, untrustworthy and psychotic.

Trace punched on the brakes. The tires squealed in protest. Then he ground the gears and wrenched the key from the ignition. For good measure, he slammed the door.

Then he scowled at himself. Who was the one banging, stomping, and slamming around like a mad man?

Of course he was mad! Not just mad—furious!

How long had Freddie planned to seduce him to her bed under the pretense of being someone else? And then really fuck with his mind with her split personality act? How long would it have been before she'd invited Mr. Hair for a threesome? She was probably in the middle of orgies every night back in L.A.

She and her punk boyfriend were probably having a big laugh at his expense right now. Then they'd forget him and hunt fresh meat.

His heart wrenched for her family. They couldn't replace a daughter and sister so easily. He hoped his patient didn't suffer a relapse.

He let himself into his practice, flipped on the late night news, and plopped onto the long leather couch in his private office.

Stretching out, he shielded his eyes from the harsh light with his arm. Still too bright, he flipped the switch with his foot.

The television glowed eerily in the room, mocking him.

He was drifting off to sleep when the newscaster mentioned Skye Blue and Thunder. Perking up, he increased the volume and gazed raptly at the hypnotic screen.

"Mrs. Carly Keith has just named her husband's long-time lover Skye Blue, aka Wenefred Applegate, as co-defendant in her multi-million-dollar divorce suit."

The allegation roared in his head. His blood boiled and his stomach lurched. Pain shredded his heart that he could love a woman who didn't hold marriage sacred.

Love? He growled. How could he love Freddie Applegate or Skye Blue? And if he loved one of them, which one?

He groaned and massaged his throbbing head. He didn't want to love either one of them. He didn't want to be within ten miles of them.

Them? He meant her. Now, she had driven him as nuts as she was. His head was splitting in two, a perfect match for his heart.

Wendy's face flickered on screen, and he lost it. Unable to look at her, he hurled the remote at the TV.

* * * * *

A knock rapped on the front door at the ungodly hour of eleven A.M. Wendy was the only one fully awake and dressed decently. That was because she hadn't been able to sleep and hadn't bothered changing into nightclothes. But she had a phobia about answering the door or phone.

"For heaven's sake, see who it is." Lightning hadn't closed his eyes till five A.M. and he looked worse than death, his hair tangled and matted.

"Look out the window first. Make sure it's not an army of press again," Hail said sleepily, rubbing her eyes with her fists. Mascara smeared under her lashes across the bridge of her nose.

Wendy shook her head. "I'm not getting it."

Lightning frowned and stabbed her with his steely-eyed glare. "You want me to go in my birthday suit? They'll really love that."

"That'd be a sight worse than death, seeing your hairy balls," Thunder drawled, poking his head up over the couch he'd passed out on around three in the morning.

"Oh, all right. I'll get the lousy door. But I vote we hire someone to screen the calls and the door from now on." Her flip-flops clomped on the linoleum as she plodded to the window.

"I vote we move back to my mansion in L.A., with my butler, cook, and locked iron gates that keep the crazies out." Lightning stroked his newly growing goatee, thoughtfully.

The bell shrilled again. "Pest, isn't he?" She peered through the window to check out their visitor. A sweet white-haired granny leaned on the bell. Her flowery muumuu swayed around her ankles in the breeze.

Wendy breathed a sigh of relief. "It's just an elderly woman. Wonder what she wants?"

A relief-filled smile curved Wendy's lips, and her chest loosened. She unlatched the door and opened it wide. "Hello."

"Hi, dearie. Are you Wenefred Applegate?" The little bespectacled, gnarled woman squinted up at her hopefully.

"Yes." The bright Florida sunshine filtered through a mangrove of palm trees that swayed in the slight ocean breeze, dappling the yard. The scent of saltwater and seaweed tickled her nose. "May I help you?"

The woman thrust an official looking document in her hands and her expression instantly twisted diabolically. "You've been served." The woman cackled and ambled away. "My record's unblemished. No one ever suspects me."

Thunder dove for the door, hissing obscenities. "That's from my wife, isn't it?"

Lightheaded from lack of oxygen, Wendy blinked. She shut the door, leaned against it, and then tried to absorb the content of the letter.

Thunder read over her shoulder, his expression black. "That cobra."

Wendy gulped and nodded. "She named me as co-defendant in her divorce suit. She thinks you...and I..."

"I wish. You won't sleep with me, but I'm being crucified for having an affair with you." Thunder slapped the floor resoundingly.

"We didn't do anything, she has no proof..." Wendy clawed at any bright thought, valiantly trying not to submerge into a dark morass.

Lightning snorted and rambled into the room wearing his sheet toga style. "Since when does truth and justice prevail in court anymore? My last two wives twisted everything. The judges always sided with them. You either gotta get a lot of dirt on them or settle quietly out of court and run away with your tail tucked between your legs. If I ever take the plunge again, I'm having my fiancée sign a pre-nup."

Wendy's heart sank. How many times had she denied any type of love affair with Thunder and no one believed her? "This won't hurt Storm, will it?"

"Naaa. All publicity is good publicity." Lightning's maudlin tone contrasted sharply with his peppy words.

"Time to pow wow with Rog and Celia," Rain said as she leaned against the wall and filed her nails. "Let the experts do what we pay the big bucks for."

"I'm surprised they aren't all over us already," Hail said. She poured herself a stiff Cuban coffee and downed it.

"Probably busy putting out fires. Man, you two really stirred up a hornet's nest." Lightning twisted his lips and hitched up his sheet.

His accusation stung and Wendy bared her teeth. "You three sleep with groupies all the time." She held up her forefinger. "I slept with a whole one. One I've known all my life." Loved all my life, pathetic as it was. "Now I'm the troublemaker? Excuse me if the logic of it eludes me."

"Well, if you were hussies like us, the press wouldn't have been waiting and watching for you to slip up." Rain stopped filing to glare at her.

Hail stood behind Rain, presenting a united front. Her spiked bleached hair stood out at all angels. "Yeah, they always want to nail the perfect ones."

Perfect? What a kiss of death! In their book, perfect meant prissy, better than thou. Sorrow flooded her. Now, they were turning on each other. This was no more a safe haven than her mother's house.

Wendy rose to her feet, clutching the summons. She marched to her room, grabbed her suitcase and slammed out, yelling, "I quit!" She had no clue where she was going or how she was going to get there, so she just put one foot in front of the other and followed the beach highway. Eventually, a bus or taxi would come by and she'd make her way to the airport.

Thunder ran after her, huffing, a muscle shirt baring his shoulders, his legs encased in a pair of anti-tank shorts with a screen print skull on the left leg. He blocked her path and clamped her arms in his iron grip. "You're overreacting. You're scared and hurt, running on empty. Come back and we'll all kiss and make up."

"Why? So they can insult me again. I didn't do anything to them, yet everything's my fault?" She trudged around him, her sandals crunching gravel and sand.

Seething, she turned and walked backwards. "Oh, yeah. I'm to blame for original sin, too. They're just mad that we came here because of my family emergency."

She sighed, totally exhausted in every possible way. The relentless sun beat down on her face, baking her. The calm ocean breeze provided little relief from the furnace-like heat.

"Come back. They're sorry they came down on you like that. Everyone's on edge."

"Then why aren't they out here?" She regretted her outburst and wished she could take it back. But she was tired of being the one who always backed down first, who always made amends.

"Look behind you," Thunder said softly, his eyes misting over.

She sucked in her breath. Trace! Her mother!

Holding her breath, she glanced over her shoulder. Rain, Lightning, and Hail stood there with their arms outstretched.

Hail spoke first. She had scrubbed her face clean, ran a brush through her hair, and looked more respectable. "Just because we like to be sluts doesn't mean you have to."

"We love you just the way you are," Lightning said, winking at her. He'd pulled on a t-shirt and Prana Sonora shorts. The straight cut legs and sturdy fabric made his legs look like sticks. He'd pulled his hair back into a ponytail, but the sunlight still glinted off the brassy tresses.

"Don't leave us." Rain wrung her hands together in front of her. She'd slipped into a sun suit imprinted with sea shells. "I can barely sing and Hail sounds worse than a bullfrog."

"Hey!" Hail pinched Rain hard on the meaty flesh of her arm.

"Ouch! Well, you do." Rain punched the air with her fist.

"Down girls!" Lightning stepped between them. "No warring during the peace treaty." He turned to Wendy. "Honestly, your gorgeous voice aside, which we would die without, we love you. We're family."

"And families squabble. I know. I have five sisters. Forgive us?" Rain held out her arms again and crooked her fingers for Wendy to come.

The ice melted around Wendy's heart and she ran into her friend's arms. "I love you, too." Tears stung her eyes.

Hail sniffed and enveloped both women in a hug.

"I think I'm going to cry," Thunder wiped at crocodile tears.

"Group hug!" Lightning pounced on them, almost crushing her ribs so that she gasped for air.

Not one to be left out, Thunder barreled into the fray. "We cool again?"

Wendy choked back happy tears. "Yeah, we're cool again."

Lightning scooped her up without warning and ran to the ocean with her, ignoring her loud shrieks of protest.

"Don't you dare!" She pummeled his back with her fists and flailed her legs but he didn't flinch.

Lightning's evil chuckle rasped over her. "Don't ever dare a crazy man!" He tossed her in the water, and then dove into a frothy oncoming wave.

"You bast..." Wendy splashed him, and then swallowed a mouthful of seawater when a big wave caught her off guard, knocking her from her precarious stance.

The other three rushed into the gentle waves. They frolicked until they were too tired to stand.

"Let's go home," Thunder said next to Wendy's ear.

"Do we have to?" She was chilling, floating on her back, letting the waves lull her into the most peaceful state she'd been in for a very long time.

"I mean home to L.A. Tonight. Or soon as we can catch a flight."

"What about the Savannah and Pensacola concerts?" Wendy stood up with a sigh and plucked a piece of seaweed off her arm. Gazing out at the shimmering sun resting on the glassy ocean, she shifted her feet as a sharp piece of coral stabbed the tender sole.

"That's why God created planes, luv." Thunder flapped his arms and she wondered if he knew how silly he looked, although they all looked pretty ridiculous jumping around in the ocean in their street clothes.

* * * * *

"...I love you, too." Wendy stopped dead when she heard her own voice float into the kitchen. Only she hadn't uttered a syllable. She was home alone...except for the TV.

She froze, the peanut butter bagel she'd just taken a bite of glued to the roof of her mouth. The knife she'd been holding clattered to the floor.

How could that be on the TV?

Then Carly Keith's voice followed. "See? Skye Blue and my husband declaring their love for one another, caught on tape. Their denials are bogus."

Wendy's paralysis lifted and she sprinted to see the so-called damning evidence. She perched on the glass coffee table in front of her chrome entertainment center and turned up the volume.

She peered at Carly's smug face, chafing. "Come on, put the tape back on. I've a right to see my accuser."

Her cell phone shrilled and she grabbed it out of her pocket and flipped it open without taking her gaze off the screen.

"I'm going to kill her." Thunder had never sounded so strung out. "This is low, even for her."

"Where could they have gotten this? She'd never said that to Thunder in public.

"There must've been a hidden camera in that security vehicle that took us home from the Key West concert." Several loud thwacks made her wince as he spoke. He must be throwing darts again, probably at a picture of his wife.

Bile bubbled up in her throat. "But that's not all I said. I said 'I love you, too. As a brother'."

"Cut and paste, luv. They doctored the tape."

She wanted to murder that security guard with her bare hands. She massaged her temples and tried to think clearly. "Can't your lawyer subpoena the entire tape? Then we'll show the whole thing in court to prove our innocence."

A deep guttural growl rumbled over the line. "Do you think they'd turn over that part? I guarantee it's long gone. Besides, what I said damns me."

So true. "Can't you settle out of court like Lightning advised?" She rose to her full height as her butt was getting numb.

"She's out for blood — yours and mine."

Wendy wanted to scream but paced the room instead. She wandered out to her balcony and gazed out over the Valley, but the twinkling lights failed to lift her spirits. "Why mine? If she saw that tape, she knows I'm not a threat."

"But you have something she never can — my heart."

The pathos in her best friend's voice about tore her in two. Unrequited love was a bitch. She knew too well. So was guilt. She hated being the cause of any of Thunder's pain.

She laughed without mirth. They were quite a pair. "So, what are we going to do?"

"I don't know. Roger wants us to air it on TV. Whether we're believed or not, it's publicity. I'll need all the money I can get to pay her lousy alimony and my attorney's fees."

"I wish there was more I could do. Perhaps if I talk to her, woman to woman..."

"No! She'll twist anything you say. Stay far away from her and talk when Roger and Celia give you permission."

Were they back in kindergarten? "Let's set up a conference call with them tomorrow. I can't take any more tonight."

"Uh...does that mean you've seen the headlines?"

Oh no! "I was getting ready to eat my dinner and read the paper when you called."

"Well, she got to the press, too. They're not pretty. Be warned."

Of course not. This must be the legendary price of fame. Damn, inflation was high!

"You'll get through this. We're all on your side. Get some rest now." She doubted she could take her own advice, not with her nerves so jumpy. She itched to see the headlines.

"I could rest better in your bed, in your arms."

She expelled a long sigh. "It's saying things like that that has you in this mess. For all we know, these lines are bugged. You'd best be a lot more careful." She wished him goodnight and closed her phone, feeling like a hypocrite.

Good night? It was just the opposite. She went in search of the two daily papers she subscribed to and flipped through them. She spied her face splashed all over the front page in the entertainment section. The bold headline seemed to jump out at her. 'Is Thunder In The Skye?'

Revolting!

The second paper wasn't any better. 'Thunder Jumps Skye'. She moaned and ripped the sickening articles full of lies and insinuations into a thousand tiny pieces.

* * * * *

The next morning, they met with Roger and Celia in Celia's office.

"This calls for some serious damage control, darlings. You two should not be seen together, except in concert or rehearsal, until after the divorce is finalized. Don't even think about walking out of here together. Don't call each other on the phone. Don't email each other." Celia blew ringlets of smoke toward the side and crushed her cigarette into her marble ashtray. Then she tucked her silvery blond shoulder-length hair behind her diamond-studded ears.

Roger swiveled his piercing gaze on Thunder as he tugged his PDA out of his pink and beige plaid shirt pocket. "Don't be seen with any woman. Not even your maid."

Lights danced in Celia's silvery-blue icy eyes as she regarded Skye. "Now, if you were to be seen around town a lot with a handsome young hottie, that would go a long way in alleviating the rumors and accusations about the two of you." The PR mogul scribbled notes in her journal with her platinum pen.

Roger leaned forward, punching his PDA keyboard, his shoulders hunched. "What about that doctor dude that always dressed in leather? Can't you pal around with him? That would get some of the heat off Carly's accusations about the two of you."

Celia's eyes glazed pewter. "Oh, yeah. He's a real hottie. I'd love to meet him…I mean do a PR work up with the two of you." She rubbed her highly polished nail with her thumb as she let her discerning gaze rake over Wendy.

Jealousy shot through Wendy white and hot. But she forced her blood pressure down. Trace didn't belong to her. He never would. He'd made that clear enough. He couldn't even stand to look at her or hear her name. She had no right to be jealous.

"That's old news, darling," she drawled, acting as nonchalant as she could, even as her heart contracted so sharply she could hardly exhale. "He's history."

"You sure? He's such a cutie." Celia failed to sound the least bit sad.

Wendy had to pull in her claws and force a smile to her face. "Absolutely. Sorry I can't help that way."

"Oh, but you still can! We'll pair you up with another hot young stud who also needs publicity. How old are you? Forty? Forty-five?"

Wendy frowned. *Did she really look so old? Why did that matter?* She gritted her teeth. "Twenty-eight."

"Oh, is that all?" Now, disappointment clouded her saccharine voice. "You know those May-December romances are all over the news right now. You really should use a better skin regime. I'll give you the number of my cosmetologist. She can work miracles."

Wendy's eyes widened. What a slap in the face! She needed a miracle? Enough with the personal remarks already! So, she wasn't Helen of Troy or even Cinderella. She wasn't the Bride of Frankenstein, either.

She scraped her chair back so fast it toppled over. "Okay, I'll keep my distance and abandon my friend till after his divorce is final. Happy?" She slipped her purse strap over her shoulder and turned to leave.

"Don't leave yet, Wendy. I'm sure Celia didn't mean to sound so rude and insensitive, did you, Celia?" Roger glared at the publicist, twin spots of cherry red heating his cheeks.

The woman swallowed her catty grin and instilled warmth into her tone. "Of course I didn't mean it that way. No harm, no foul. Sit down and let's talk about our first plan of action, and then we'll find a good match for you. Who knows? Maybe it'll turn into a real love match like Brad and Jen."

She was through with love!

Thunder picked up her chair and held it for her as she smoothed her shorts beneath her.

Roger frowned and shook his head at the musician.

Obviously, being a gentleman was out for the present also.

"Uh huh," she mumbled, totally against such blatant lies even to help her friend. Even lies made with the best intentions tended to blow up in one's face. And she didn't need any more wounds. She was raw enough.

"So, what is it?" Thunder twirled his hair, golden fire glinting off the silky strand.

"A TV interview by Diane Sampson. Storm will burst out of the closet. She's an old friend from college. She's fair and tough, but she won't pull any tricks. You're scheduled to appear next Tuesday."

Wendy smoothed her shorts over her knees. "In or out of costume?"

"Since it's taped ahead, why not both? They'll show a clip of you performing your latest hit. Then we'll show you coming out of makeup, and then she'll interview you in your regular dress, no costume."

"I'm not really comfortable appearing without the costume..." She wasn't Helen of Troy, remember? According to Celia, she was Methuselah's mother.

"Oh! Before I forget as I know she'll ask you, are you a lesbian?"

Wendy blinked. Fury flashed through her. Everybody thought her a lesbian and Thunder's soul mate simultaneously. Someone please deliver her! "No. Are they going to ask Hail and Rain that, too? Or Thunder and Lightning if they're gay? Or am I being singled out? If so, why?"

"Well, it's those recent headlines. Rumors don't die easily." Celia scratched more notes in her hateful journal.

Hello! As her PR agent, Celia should already know the answer to that one. "That stupid reporter insinuated I was having an affair with myself. A little impossible if you ask me." Even if she really did have a split personality.

"Right...We'll have those photos blown up. Just keep your cool and that'll be a non-issue." Celia tapped her pen on the desk. "Now, one of my clients was just dumped by his very famous girlfriend. I think you'd two hit it off famously."

"Smashing." Thunder sounded less than thrilled.

Wendy rolled her eyes. She hoped this lothario didn't have a mirror fetish.

* * * * *

Trace tried to forget Wendy, to exorcise her from his heart. But reminders were everywhere.

Her voice sang to him over the radio. He could still see her gazing at him as she sang about love lost and two souls forever joined.

With a grimace, he switched stations. Another Storm song pierced the night, and he stabbed the radio off and drove the rest of the way to the gym in silence.

He had been lifting weights for about half an hour, when Wendy's face flashed on the small TV mounted on the wall. "Storms's lead singer Skye Blue, recently unmasked as Wenefred Applegate, has been named as a co-defendant in the divorce filed by Carly Keith, estranged wife of Ian Keith, better known as Thunder."

Trace lost his concentration and dropped the weight nearly crushing his toe.

One of his old schoolmates, Rob Clemmons, who looked like he'd stepped out of an Arabian Night's tale with his clean-shaven head, goatee, and muscular physique, elbowed him in the ribs. "Quiet waters run deep, don't they? That Wendy Applegate has sure caused a mess of trouble, hasn't she? You believe this?"

"No." *Yes, but he wished he didn't.*

"Never would've thought it. "His old friend regarded him quizzically. "Have you known long she was this famous rock star?"

Trace swallowed hard. "Not a clue." Hell, he'd believed her line about being a traveling feminine hygiene product salesman. He couldn't be a bigger idiot.

"This was taken by a hidden video camera," the exotic brunette newscaster said.

Trace couldn't tear his eyes from the coming train wreck. Thunder cupped Wendy's face and caressed her lips with his. "I think we'd make a happy pair." The punker gazed deeply into Wendy's eyes, hope blazing. Wendy stroked Thunder's face lovingly. "I love you."

The camera panned back in on the newscaster. "And there you have it. A heart wrenching declaration of love. Beautiful if not for the fact, one of them is married to another. I'd hate to be his wife and have to watch this."

"Yep," Trace said. Or her ex and listen to her declaring her love for another. It sucked.

So, she'd lied about loving him and not loving Thunder, just as he'd suspected. His own eyes and ears didn't deceive him.

"Hey, you okay, Doc?" Rob waved a beefy hand in front of Trace's face.

"Yeah." *Sure.* Wendy had not only trampled his heart but she'd done it on national TV. He couldn't watch another minute.

"Catch you later." He stood under the gym's shower just long enough to let the warm water sluice him off. And then he retreated into the night. But he could swear her reflection mocked him in the glass door as he slammed out. *Was no place sacred?* She invaded his home, his office, his car, and now his gym.

He stared up at the moonlight and swore that her face stared down at him from the clouds. *He was losing it.*

Chapter Thirteen

Tension sizzled in the air, or perhaps just in Wendy's soul. The performance in costume went well for the Diane Sampson show, but sour milk curdled in her stomach as Diane's camera crews filmed the band coming out of makeup. Unlike their normal routine of removing their own makeup, professional cosmetologists performed the task this time, creaming face cleanser over her, and then wiping it off carefully. She felt like an expensive Barbie doll.

Diane Sampson, the internationally renowned journalist, stuck close to Wendy's side throughout the ordeal, making Wendy want to scream. It wasn't that the polished woman was unkind or rude. But why was she being singled out? She didn't kid herself that she was any more important than the rest of the band, and she hoped no one saw her that way. They were a family and they didn't need any dissension. The day the process server had dumped the summons on her had been their one and only flirtation with breaking up. She never wanted to go through that again.

She shivered from the memory, but quickly quelled her reaction lest the camera pick it up.

"How do you feel about coming out of the closet, Skye? I may call you Skye?" Diane scooted up, cozy, as if they were old friends. The interviewer was splendid in her cashmere empire dress that hugged her perfect size two figure lovingly. It matched her mint green eyes and complimented the highlights in her russet bob.

She preferred Wendy, but since her fans thought of her as Skye, that would do. "I'd be honored if you did. May I call you Diane?"

Diane's lips curved upward in a genuinely warm smile. "I insist that you do." She encouraged Wendy to spill her guts.

"It's scary coming out of the closet. I'll never be able to mingle with society anonymously again."

"Have you had problems with that since coming out?" Shadows flickered across Diane's eyes. Genuine concern etched itself across her ordinary features.

"A bit. I can't just answer my door at home anymore. I've had to hire a maid. I've had to hire a car, driver, and security so I can go out in public. I hope that's only temporary as I enjoy my freedom."

"Please believe me when I say I understand. It's nice to be loved by our public, but too much love isn't a good thing either." Diane licked her glossy lips and sat up straight.

"Precisely." Wendy tossed the camera a winning smile to soften her words. "We love our fans and we know we couldn't have made it to this level without them. But like everyone, sometimes we just need some peace and quiet."

"Some people say you wore makeup because you're insecure about the way you look. I must tell you on the record, that I don't agree. You're a very lovely person, in or out of makeup." Diane's kind words took her by surprise, ameliorating some of the pain her brotherhood of the press had inflicted recently. Of course, Diane probably understood, as she didn't possess classic beauty either. The journalist was striking, graceful, and poised. Well-groomed and polished, she was very attractive even with a too-square chin and too narrowly set eyes. Some of Wendy's courage crept back.

Wendy's long-time pain ebbed away, and she found herself wanting to open up to this woman. "Yes, such insinuations have been flying about since we came out. A couple of your brethren actually told me straight out that my younger sister, who just won the crown of Miss Florida, by the way, and is an extraordinarily beautiful woman, is much more beautiful than me. That I'm basically a dog in comparison."

Shock danced in Diane's eyes as she gasped. "How cruel. I hope you don't believe them."

"I think I grew up believing that. It's tough growing up with a beauty queen in the family, especially if you're merely ordinary." Wendy's soul came pouring forth. It was so easy to talk to Diane. The woman made her feel secure, and she couldn't help but open up and share her deepest, darkest secrets. *No wonder she was so successful.*

"Do you really think of yourself as ordinary?" Diane's eyes narrowed on her and she held the mike back out to her.

"On my good days. Like I said, it's hard. I grew up being second best." *At best.* "All of Angelina's pageant pursuits came first. Mine took a back seat. She's the star in our house. I was invisible."

"And you liked being invisible? Otherwise, why hide yourself under your costumes? I'd think you'd want to stand up and be counted. You have a beautiful gift. You should never feel second rate." Diane sounded more like a psychologist now than a talk-show host. And as tough as she was, as surprisingly correct, Wendy found she didn't mind.

"I didn't think so," Wendy said thoughtfully. "But now that we've come out of the closet so to speak, I'm quite shy about showing my real face to the world."

"You're not shy with me. You're perfectly delightful to the contrary. Although I want you to promise me you'll value your own worth more." Diane admonished her gently, like an older sister would. "You have one of the most beautiful voices I've ever heard. You and Storm are a mega success."

"Thank you. I just hope our fans aren't angry with us for what some have called a major deception." Wendy couldn't believe she'd just divulged this.

"I hate to ask this, but I know our viewers want to hear it from your own mouth." Diane shifted on her stool uncomfortably and her dangling high-heeled foot stopped bouncing.

Wendy winced inside, erecting the wall around her heart. She'd been drilling herself in front of the mirror for all the possible hideous questions Diane might ask.

"You've been accused of being a lesbian. Are you?"

Wendy crossed her chest mentally, seeking higher guidance and grace. "No. I like men very much."

"But those pictures of a woman sneaking out of your hotel room late at night? Why was she there then, if she wasn't your lover? You have to admit that was a strange time to be sneaking out of your room, in the middle of the night." Diane's brows quirked and she didn't give an inch.

Celia motioned for Wendy to smile from the sidelines. She'd also been coaching Wendy on answers to the obvious questions. They'd been over this one about a thousand times.

Roger stood beside her, visibly quaking, more so than he'd ever done at a performance. His nervousness made her jumpy, so she focused back on Celia's cool demeanor.

"Those were pictures of me without my makeup. I was sneaking out to catch a breath of fresh air or a midnight snack. So unless I'm sleeping with myself—which would be impossible, the photographers didn't discover anything." Wendy winked for the camera.

Hail brought the enlarged photos over to be shown on television and modeled them for the camera. She pointed out Wendy's face as Wendy stood next to it for comparison.

"See? I'm the mystery woman."

Diane clucked appreciatively. "So, I see. And you have the last laugh—all the way to the bank."

Wendy nodded to Hail who discreetly disappeared with the evidence. "Yes, I do." *Only about that.*

The makeup artist finished with removing her makeup and they regrouped in Diane's comfy lobby in front of a full audience. Hail and Rain flanked her as Roger and Celia had arranged. Thunder and Lightning bookended them, and they all faced Diane and the audience.

"So, what do you have to say about coming out?" Diane asked the group in general. "Was Skye the only one in favor of using costumes and painting your faces?"

Lightning sat forward, the static electricity in his hair making it pouf out wildly. "I rather enjoyed playing dress up. It was cool emulating one of my all-time favorite bands. It worked for them, so we figured it could work for us and it did."

Rain piped up. "The makeup gave me a rash, so no, I didn't enjoy getting in costume. But it's part of the gimmick and I can afford a dermatologist. I think I keep him in his Rolls Royce all by my lonesome."

Diane smiled. "Now maybe you won't have to wear it so much." She held out the mike again. "Did you let your families and close friends know about your alter egos and double life?" She went down the line in turn, starting with Lightning.

Lightning and Hail said yes, their families knew. So, Wendy was in the unenviable position of being the only one who hadn't informed her family. She swallowed hard and stilled her twitching fingers. "No. I didn't tell anyone, except for the band, our manager, and publicist. As we discussed earlier, I preferred total anonymity."

"So, how are they taking it now? Is it correct that you were dragged out of the closet the day your sister was crowned Miss Florida?" Diane leaned in close to Wendy again, her eyes glittering.

Wendy's pulse raced, the vein in her wrist aching. "Not well, I'm afraid. And it was horrible timing. I never wanted to disrupt or cloud my sister's big day. I hope some day she'll forgive me."

Diane patted her hand sisterly. "I hope so, too. Surely once the hurt has settled down, she'll see that. And that gives us the perfect segue into our film clip of that day."

Thunder shot up out of his chair. "What clips? You're not going to air those here?"

Roger joined them onstage, introduced himself briefly, and put a calming hand on Thunder's shoulder. He murmured in a low voice to the guitarist, so that Wendy couldn't hear their conversation.

The film lit up the projection screen behind them, so Wendy twisted around to view it and moaned. Not that one. Hypnotized, she couldn't tear her gaze away.

Reporters mobbed herself and Thunder. Her heart shriveled as they made their rude observations about how homely she was, especially in comparison to her sister. And then she witnessed the rerun of Thunder punching out the reporter who had dared ask him how he could leave his exquisite wife for such a sow. It took all her courage to hold her head up through it a second time.

"How ghastly." Diane clicked her tongue and shook her head. "Dreadful."

The interviewer turned to Thunder. "Even if we hadn't heard you profess your love for Skye, your defense of her would lead us to believe the depth of your feelings for her. What have you to say?"

Thunder started to scowl and then schooled his features into a cool mask. "Gentlemen don't treat ladies that way and Skye is one of the grandest ladies I know. The man deserved far worse than a punch to the nose. No one says that to Skye and gets away with it. I wouldn't stand by and let any man put down any woman thus."

"How honorable of you. You're an endangered breed—regular white knight in shining armor." Diane's fingers curled tighter about her microphone and she inched closer. "So, is your wife wrong? You don't love Skye?" She ran the hidden video clip of Thunder and Skye in the security car where he professed his love for her.

"I love Skye. But she doesn't love me…except as a best friend or a brother." Thunder laughed wryly at himself.

"Once, a long time ago, I had a small piece of Skye's heart, but she's always truly belonged to another with whom I can't seem to compete."

Wendy drew her breath in sharply and prayed Trace never saw this interview or read any articles in reference. Of course, he didn't believe she loved him, so even if he did see it, he would assume her friend lied or alluded to someone else.

Diane wheeled her chair back to Wendy, to her horror. "And who is this mystery man, Skye? Is it the famous movie star we've seen you around Hollywood with all week? You've been inseparable. Gossip is flying, you know."

Roger implored her with his eyes to say yes, but she couldn't squeeze out the lie. "No..."

To her supreme mortification, her pretend lover, darling of a new hit TV sitcom, Vincente Quintero, sauntered out of the wings. He beamed at the audience and waved his hands high in the air over his head. "Grazi, grazi!" He laid a big, wet kiss on Wendy, making her skin crawl, and then squeezed in a chair beside her. Then he captured her hand and dragged it to his lips and nuzzled it as if he couldn't get enough of her.

His overacting sickened her and it was all she could do not to snatch her hand away. So pretty for a man, he was sleazy. Slime oozed from his slick charm.

"What a pleasant surprise. Welcome, Vincente. I'm so charmed to have you join us. I'm sure our TV viewing audience is, too. I'm so blessed to be surrounded by so many handsome men today."

Oh please, don't inflate his ego any more than it already was. He was about to explode from his big head. She did not miss his slimy hand when he replaced her hand on her lap to treat Diane to a similar caress.

Diane's laughter tinkled annoyingly. Vincente seemed to have that effect on all women from the cradle to the nursing home, except for her. Even Hail and Rain had sat up straight and thrust out their chests at first sight of him. "You're a very lucky man, Vincente. I've just been getting to know your better half and she's absolutely charming."

Her so-called better half turned an adoring gaze on her and entwined his fingers through hers. "And she possesses such a bellisimo voice. She croons like songbird and charms the ferocious monster with her lullaby."

Wendy couldn't stand the fake fawning. "Oh, he's too modest. He is an absolutely wonderful actor. If you've not seen his new show, you have to tune in. It's marvelous." There, she'd done her PR duty. Now save her!

Vincente hugged her and left his arm around her shoulder. "We're so crazy in love. We're so very happy, I have to shout it to the world."

She'd get Roger and Celia for this. Her boyfriend sounded like a bad song.

"So, there's no credence in Carly Keith's allegations that her husband Ian, Thunder, is having a love affair with Skye?"

"Absolutely none. Where would they find the time? We are constantly together. She has no time, no need for another man. I satisfy her every desire, and she, my every fantasy."

Wendy moaned inside. If this was a sample of his acting, she was surprised he could make a living at it.

"So, do I hear wedding bells for the two of you in the near future?"

God no! Wendy's head was about to explode. Nothing could entice her to marry this moron. She could barely stand to break bread with him. It was all she could do not to jerk her hand away or rub his seedy kisses off her flesh.

"When and if we do, you'll be the first to know," Wendy said to Diane.

* * * * *

Trace stopped in to check on Bessie after he made his hospital rounds. "How's my most beautiful patient today?" He leaned over her bed and kissed her cheek.

"Feeling like the worst mother in the world. Have you seen the latest?" Bessie clicked the remote at her TV, switching it off.

"You mean the divorce proceedings or her new friend?" The Italian Stallion? He'd been avoiding television, radio, and newspapers. He couldn't take seeing her face everywhere he looked. Eventually, the media would tire of Wendy and her escapades.

"Did you see the Diane Sampson show?" A morose expression clouding her face, Bessie clutched the remote control.

"Only a small clip." He'd seen the part where her new boy toy was drooling all over her. How could that make his patient think she was a poor mother? Wendy was a big girl now and ruled her own love life.

"I can't believe I didn't see it all those years. I was so blind. So very blind..." A lone tear escaped Bessie's eye and trickled down her cheek.

This couldn't be the same show he had in mind. He hitched up his slacks and pulled up a chair beside her. "Would you like to talk about it?"

Bessie pointed the remote at the television and turned it on. "I'll do you one better and show you. We taped it. It had Angelina in tears. She's beside herself."

What terrible thing had Wendy said or done to cause her family new grief? He'd obviously been blinded by her, too. He obviously didn't know her anymore, didn't want to know her. His Freddie had never been unkind. She never would have hurt her family.

Bessie seemed to go into a trance when Wendy started pouring out her heart to Diane Sampson. He'd never known her to be so open or so humble. This wasn't at all what he had expected to see or hear.

His heart dove into his feet when Diane coaxed Wendy to tell her how she'd felt second rate all her life, living in the shadow of her sister's beauty and her family's total obsession with Angelina to the exclusion of Wendy and her talent.

The ice encasing his heart melted and he felt like a total cad.

"See?" Bessie rewound it and hung on every word, her tears mounting. "I can't believe I caused my own child so much pain."

He put his hand over Bessie's and confiscated the remote. "You're being too hard on yourself. I don't think you should watch this right now."

"Oh! But you have to see the rest." She snatched the black box away from him and fast-forwarded to a news clip.

Trace recognized the pageant, and narrowed his eyes. He had to strangle several rude retorts that sprung to his lips as the reporters told Wendy she was homely, and then called her a sow. He rooted for Thunder when he decked the vulgar bastard.

Then fury swelled in him and he had to choke back a growl. That should have been him putting the man in his place, protecting Wendy. And he'd abandoned her to those idiots. He had refused to listen to her, sure she was rationalizing her selfishness.

And now, she'd gone and found someone else, someone worse than the long-haired hippy. He had screwed up royally.

"What do you think?" Bessie asked, putting the TV on mute. "Angelina blames herself, but it's all mine and her father's doing. Nothing I say can console her. I've wrecked both my daughters' lives."

Trace turned off the television and removed the tape. It was going under lock and key so she wouldn't keep torturing herself. He reached in his pocket and dragged out a clean handkerchief which he used to dab her wet cheeks. "I think Wendy had the right idea. The three of you need to sit down and discuss this. Really talk."

"Her guard won't let our calls through. She won't talk to us." More tears ran down Bessie's face. She dragged out a long, crumpled envelope with postage stamps canceled. "She returned our letters, too. She doesn't want anything to do with us."

Trace swallowed a few choice curses and eyed the letter. This couldn't be allowed to go on and ruin all their lives. "May I borrow that for awhile?"

Bessie craned her neck to gaze up at him and hiccoughed. "What are you going to do with it?"

"Make things better. Don't worry how. I'll handle it." He accepted the outstretched envelope, smoothed it between his fingers, and then stuck it in his pocket.

"Are you two going to have a talk as well?" Shrewdness returned to Bessie's face as she regarded him aptly. "Maybe it's not too late. She didn't look in love with that Italian dandy to me."

Hope flared in Trace's heart. He instructed his office manager to reschedule his appointments or give them to one of his partners, and to book him on the next flight to L.A. leaving Ft. Lauderdale or West Palm Beach. It was time he and Wendy had it out, also.

Chapter Fourteen

"Fraulein Blue is not available. I tell her you call," a middle-aged German maid drill sergeant told him firmly. She closed the door and he stuck his foot inside to prevent Brunhilda from locking him out.

"Then I'll wait." Trace pushed the door open and entered Wendy's apartment despite the woman's hostile expression. He let his gaze take in the modern but comfy décor that totally contrasted with her mother's Victorian furnishings and clutter. He sank gratefully onto a buttery soft leather sofa and gave his sore feet a rest. "Please tell her Trace Cooper is here. She knows who I am."

"Fraulein not here! You leave before I call police." The woman huffed and puffed and she crossed her arms over her hefty chest. She towered over him, her feet set apart at parade rest.

"Wendy and I are old friends. I'm sure she won't mind that I'm here. But if it makes you feel better, call her and she'll tell you."

The little rotund attack maid snarled at him. "You're on the no contact list. You leave now."

"Along with her mother and sister?" He bristled at the servant's imperious tone and vowed to come out triumphant. Too much was at stake to be scared off by a surly manservant. "I guess you'll just have to have me dragged out, then." He hoped his bluff worked. He didn't relish getting a police record for breaking and entering.

"No more warnings…"

The doorknob rattled and the maid sighed heavily. "Pesky reporters won't leave us alone. They swarm all over like killer bees, spreading their lies like pollen."

A woman's voice tinkled with silvery laughter and his heart stopped. He'd know that sound anywhere. Wendy was here and she sounded a lot happier than the last time he'd spoken to her, when he'd kicked her out of her own house. He moaned inwardly. How could he have been such an insensitive oaf?

He swallowed his pride and stood, ignoring Wendy's private Gestapo.

"Leave out back door." The feisty woman tried to push him out the door.

He refused to budge until he spoke to Wendy.

Wendy traipsed in swinging several shopping bags, still laughing, the handsome Vincente on her heels. She stopped dead when she spied Trace. All joy drained from her face and her musical laughter died with it. "Hello, Trace. You're a long way from home."

Primitive emotions coursed through him at the sight of the other man touching Wendy intimately. How could she have hooked up with him so fast? His muscles went on red alert.

"He barged in and won't leave. I threatened with police, but he insists he speak with you. Says he's an old friend." The maid punctuated her sentence with a harrumph and positioned herself between himself and Wendy.

Vincente squared his shoulders and looked down his hawklike nose at Trace. Then he cracked his knuckles. "I can make him leave if you wish it."

Trace stood his ground and stared at the vision before him as she placed her packages on the glass and chrome coffee table that separated him from the matching chrome entertainment center. "We really need to talk. I came a long way."

Worry pooled in the depth of her lovely eyes. "Is it Mom? Has something happened to her?"

"We need to discuss her. In private." He glared at the bodyguard.

Wendy regarded him solemnly for several seconds. "It's okay. He's my mother's doctor."

Just her mother's physician? That's not how she had regarded him two months ago.

"Then certainly I should stay with you in case it's bad news." Vincente came up behind her and laid a possessive hand on her shoulder.

A growl rumbled in Trace's throat. He hated other men touching Wendy.

* * * * *

Wendy sighed and reeled on the annoying Vincente. She was so tired of this act! Or puppy love, or whatever twisted thing it had turned out to be. "Would you give it up already, Romeo? Stop acting like you're my boyfriend, like we're anything to each other."

"But I am your boyfriend. I should be here to support and help you in time of trouble." Vincente glared at Trace and his fingers bit angrily into her shoulders.

"I'm her boyfriend," Trace said through gritted teeth, stealing her breath.

When had the making up part happened? Why this abrupt about face? Excitement rattled inside her, tempered with a good amount of skepticism. "What are you talking about? You said you wanted nothing more to do with me."

Vincente puffed out his impressive chest and stepped between them. "I get rid of this loser for you. You deserve better."

Yes, she deserved better than either of them. But she'd settle for a little sanity right now and a few answers.

"Stay back, Hercules," Trace said. He looked deceptively slender in his suit jacket, but Wendy knew he had more muscles than this pumped-up steroid phony.

"Then you leave." Vincente obviously thought himself the superior the way he lifted his chin, bared his teeth, and stepped forward. He shoved Trace. "Now what you going to do?"

"I warned you." Trace threw a punch in the man's face, knocking him across the room.

Wendy gasped and ran to the injured man. She glared up at Trace, and then checked the actor for lumps and contusions. A shiner was already bruising the flesh beneath his eye. "Why'd you do that? It's just a PR stunt to get the heat off Thunder and I."

"So, you and Thunder are still together?" Trace barely sounded civilized. He strode over and towered over them. "Let me take a look at him."

Seething, Wendy moved out of the way. "First you deck them, then you doctor them?"

"I lost my cool, okay? All I wanted to do was talk to you…protect you," Trace mumbled.

Wendy strained to hear the almost inarticulate words. Surprise echoed through her and she stilled Trace's hand. "Protect me? From what?"

Trace rocked back on his haunches and sifted his fingers through his hair. "I saw that tape where Thunder decked the reporter who insulted you. That should have been me defending you."

She held her breath, unable to believe her ears. Finally she expelled it and whispered, "Why? I thought you didn't believe me? I made a fool of you."

Trace glanced down at the man who was beginning to wake up. "He'll be okay." He instructed the maid, "Help him to the couch and give him some pain reliever and a cold compress. He'll be okay."

Wendy chewed her lower lip. "Why?" she asked again, needing to know, hope flaring in her heart.

"In private. Where's the bedroom? Does the door lock?"

She nodded, unable to utter a sound. So, she pointed and led the way.

He followed her in and then locked the door. Then he folded his arms across his chest. "You do deserve better. I should have been the one protecting you because I love you. You Wendy, whether you're masquerading as Skye Blue, punk rocker, or you're the girl-next-door." She yearned to throw herself in his arms and drink of his lips, but she dare not yet. She needed to know more. "Really? But why the change of heart?"

His cheeks suffused a deep, brick red and he massaged his neck. "I didn't fully understand until I watched that tape of you on the Diane Sampson show and at the pageant, just what you've had to go through, what drove you to act as you did. I know now and it's tearing me up that I've caused some of that pain."

She inched towards him but didn't reach out. It seemed as if an invisible, impenetrable wall stood between them. "I tried to tell you, but it's not easy for me. I love my parents and sister and that would have been betraying them. I'm only good at expressing myself in song."

"And I was too stubborn, too jealous to listen. Every time I saw you with Thunder, I saw red. I couldn't think straight. I just wanted to drag you off to my cave and have you all to myself. Only I knew I couldn't take you away from your adoring fans and your glamorous life. What can I offer you that you don't already have? I'm just a simple country doctor."

Like working in smoky, alcohol-scented coliseums was fun? Or traveling so much she couldn't remember which town she was in? "I don't care about that superficial stuff. But Angelina would make a much more ideal doctor's wife than I ever could." She turned her back on him, her heart breaking again. She'd temporarily forgotten how unsuitable she was in the wife department, at least for a respectable doctor. "She's beautiful, poised, and graceful." All the things she wasn't.

"I don't know that she's any more beautiful, poised, or graceful than you. Certainly not as talented or successful." His eyes darkened with pride on her.

Surely she misread them? Hope brewed in her core. Did he appreciate her for who she was and not what she looked like?

Her legs wobbled and wouldn't hold her up much longer. "This is silly. The bed doesn't bite. I'm going to sit. Suit yourself."

She kicked off her shoes, climbed onto the middle of her bed, and crossed her legs Indian style. She folded her hands in her lap and waited for him to make the next move.

Perching on the edge of her bed, Trace twisted toward her. "You need to talk to your mother and sister. They're distraught that you won't take their calls or letters."

What in the world was he talking about? She shook her head to get the cobwebs out. Maybe she hadn't heard right. "What do you mean? They've not called or written."

Trace delved around in his pocket and extracted a crumpled envelope and tossed it on her lap. "What do you call this then?"

She picked it up and turned it over in her hands. Bold but squiggly, her mother's script stared up at her. Bright red ink postal stamps declared 'Return to Sender – Not accepted by addressee'. The post date read only a week before. She felt ill. "I swear, I never got this. I've never seen it before."

Trace removed his jacket and tossed it over the corner armoire. Then he undid a couple of buttons as if that would allow him to breathe easier.

It did just the opposite for her. The temperature in the room jumped a good twenty degrees and perspiration dotted her upper lip. She forced herself to pick a neutral spot to gaze upon, anywhere but at that enticing, but illegal triangle of hair that protruded through the vee in his open shirt.

"Then who did?"

She shrugged and turned her palms toward the ceiling. "I don't know. Maybe it was a postal error."

Trace sighed and leaned heavily on the bed, resting his head on his hand. "I might think that if that was the only returned letter. But there's a whole slew of them."

Her pulse jumped in her neck. What was going on? She crossed her heart. "Believe me. I didn't see any letters. Someone must have intercepted them. But who?"

"You okay in there, Fraulein Blue? The cops is on their way," Mrs. Klabermeier said as she pounded on the door.

Comprehension dawned in Trace's eyes the moment the truth clicked in her mind. "The maid!" they hissed simultaneously.

"Has she been screening your calls?"

Wendy's head ached and she massaged her forehead. What an idiot she'd been! "Yes. Roger employed her. He must have instructed her to keep all this from me."

"Tell this Roger guy to call off his watch dog. Who the hell is Roger?" Trace leapt to his feet and paced the room, punching his own hand.

"Our manager. He's well meaning, but tends to go overboard." She hoped he had her best interests at heart anyway.

"Oh, yeah. I'd say he did." He stopped in front of her row of Grammy awards and didn't say anything.

Alarmed when he remained silent several minutes, she crawled off the bed and joined him. Licking her suddenly dry lips, she asked, "Do those intimidate you?" She screwed up her courage. "Do I?"

He didn't look at her immediately, just continued to stare. Then he went to pick one up and stilled his hand midway. "May I?"

She nodded, wishing she could read his mind and tap into his emotions.

He turned it over in his hand, examining its splendor. Then he tested its weight in his hands. "Impressive." He turned a speculative gaze on her and let it rake slowly down her length. "I suppose it's a fever in your blood?"

Heat suffused her body, and her pussy twitched when his feverish gaze lingered at the juncture of her thighs several excruciating moments. She licked her lips, unable to concentrate on his question. She wondered what his true question was? "Wh-what?"

"Performing."

As in performing on the bed? It had been ages since she'd performed for him and her clit throbbed, longing to feel the flick of his tongue. This was too dangerous. "This is a bad place to talk. There's a beautiful view of the Valley from my balcony…"

When she went to unlock the door and escape, he caught her wrist in his steely grasp. "I love the view."

She couldn't exhale as the import of his words sank in, as he dragged her against him and teased her lips with his intoxicating kisses. "How do you know? You've not seen it yet."

His fingertips caressed her exposed flesh where her blouse dipped low, revealing an extensive amount of cleavage. Tingles shot up her spine and she squirmed against him.

Against her lips, he murmured, "Oh yes I have and it's breath-taking. I can't wait to see it again." He sucked her lower lip into his mouth and nibbled it as his hand dipped inside her shirt. He found her pebbled nipple which he kneaded between his fingers, eliciting a moan from her very core.

She writhed against him. "So, what are we going to do about my condition, Doctor?"

"What condition?"

"I'm so hot and so horny, I'm about to burn up. I've not been made love to in almost two months." Not since the last time they had been together.

He backed her against the bed until her knees buckled and she fell backwards onto the mattress, mussing the black satin sheets. Pulling up her blouse and her bra in one slick movement, he buried his face in her chest and trailed liquid fire with his tongue. "I think the only prescription for that is to fuck you until neither of us can move anymore. And then to carry you off and marry you so we can make love all day and all night no matter who gossips about us. Think you can stand it?"

On fire, she writhed against him, pushing her breast into his mouth. "Are there any side effects I should know about?"

He lifted his head and devilish merriment flickered deep in his eyes. Gently, he brushed stray tendrils of hair away from her eyes and kissed the tip of her other nipple, making her shiver deliciously. "Oh, maybe one or two. Or three."

A furnace exploded inside her and her cheeks burned. Her juices flowed and her panties became suddenly very damp. "Oh." She slipped his buttons from their loop holes, pulled the shirt tails from his slacks, and then pushed the sleeves off his arms. He had the most beautiful chest, one she wanted to mold her heart against forever. She pressed her ear to his chest and listened to his strong, but erratic heartbeat.

His chuckle was a deep masculine sound that enraptured her. She could listen to it forever and never grow tired of it.

He gazed deeply into her eyes while his hands kneaded her waist and her nipples teased his bare chest. "So?"

"So?" Had he officially asked her to marry him? She couldn't stand the embarrassment or pain if he hadn't and she accepted.

"What's ahead for us? Will you be able to fit me into your schedule?"

The devil entered her and she trailed her hand down his side, seeking his bulging cock, and released it from its cloth prison. She tugged it towards her gently. "You fit extremely well."

He growled and divested himself of his remaining clothes, letting them pool on the floor. "Is that an invitation?"

She nodded eagerly, anxious to try him on again. It had been much too long since she had sheathed his long, hard cock in her folds. She lifted her hips and struggled to remove her annoying lower coverings. "Help me."

"A gentleman always helps a lady." He wiggled his eyebrows at her and then kissed his way down her belly, paused at her waist, and then dragged her panties off with his teeth.

Damn, she had trained him well. She tried to swallow a grin and failed. "Then fuck me. Now." Her pussy quivered at the sight of his swollen cock poised over her. She curled her fingers around his girth and gently tugged it toward her until the tip parted her velvety lips.

Rapturous waves undulated through her and she bit her lip, trying to hold back. She wanted to come with him.

She met him thrust for thrust, grinding her hips against his, greedy to fill herself with his length. Her nails raked his back, as they slid against the satiny, erotic sheets.

"God, I missed you. I don't know how I was so blind I couldn't see you were Skye Blue." His words came out husky, melting against her lips.

"You did, deep down." Now, she was sure of it. He was drawn to her essence, her soul, not just to her outer shell. She had the answer that had troubled them for so long.

He lifted his weight from her and held himself in a suspended pushup so he could gaze into her eyes. "When did you get so smart?"

She squeezed his shaft with her inner folds, eliciting a moan from him. "I'm the smart, talented one, remember?" Not to mention the horny one.

He frowned at her even as he stroked into her again. "You're also the gorgeous one, inside and out."

It was her turn to pause. At this rate, they'd never climax, but then again, they'd draw out this unbelievably incredible pleasure all night...or until the police broke down the door. "Do you honestly mean it?"

He nodded slowly, deliberately. "I never say anything I don't mean." He lowered his head and drank of her lips, his tongue delving deeply inside.

Her tongue dueled with his until she broke the kiss to gasp for air. The fire stoked in her belly and she was about to explode. She squeezed him so tightly, she could feel every contour of his beautiful cock. Lava flowed freely through her veins, building to a crescendo.

Fireworks burst inside her. Brilliant reds, blues, and purples swirled before her eyes, and then Trace's smiling face slowly came into focus.

They held each other for several long moments until their breathing evened out.

"We still have a problem." His troubled gaze bore into her as he brushed her breast with the back of his hand.

"Which is?" Her throat constricted and she could barely breathe again. She knew this had been too good to be true. She must have been dreaming. Maybe she was delusional.

"You live in California. I live in Florida, on the opposite coast. What are we going to do about it?"

She sucked in her breath. How could she have forgotten so easily? She'd been thinking long and hard about this. She was getting too old to enjoy the gypsy life. It had been fun for a time, but living out of suitcases in nameless towns had lost its allure. "I've been thinking of retiring. Or at least slowing down."

Passion darkened his eyes. "You'd give up your career for me?"

She nodded slowly. "If you want me to." Her success was nice, but rather hollow without the man she'd loved all her life at her side, in her arms, and in her bed.

Then he shook his head. "It's enough that you're willing to do so. But I don't want you to give up your music or the band. It's part of you."

Confused, she peered up at him. "Then what? We'll just get together a couple of times a year, whenever I have a concert in your part of the country, or when you can get away from your practice?" *Emotional Siberia.*

He put his finger under her chin and tipped her face up, forcing her gaze to meet his. "I'll move out here to be with you."

Joyfully surprised, she blinked up at him. "But your patients. Your practice…"

"I can practice medicine anywhere. My patients will be in good hands with my partners. You, sweet songbird, are my number one priority. I can't get enough of you, Skye Blue." He rolled over onto his back and pulled her into his embrace so that his heart beat strongly against hers.

Trace dragged his cell phone from his pocket, hit speed dial, and held it out to her as she frowned in puzzlement. "Here. Time to make up with your family. Angel can't be maid of honor if you're not speaking."

Wiping a tear from her cheek, smiling tremulously at her love, Wendy accepted the phone. Joyous, her heart lighter than it had been in weeks, she squeezed Trace's warm hand. "I love you, Mom."

The End

About the author:

Ashley Ladd lives in South Florida with her husband, five children, and beloved pets. She loves the water, animals (especially cats), and playing on the computer.

She's been told she has a wicked sense of humor and often incorporates humor and adventure into her books. She also adores very spicy romance which she also weaves into her stories.

Ashley Ladd welcomes mail from readers. You can write to her c/o Ellora's Cave Publishing at 1337 Commerce Drive, Suite 13, Stow OH 44224.

Enjoy this excerpt from:
CARBON COPY

Rough, the guard chained Siobhan's hands behind her back, clasped a metal ring around her neck, and hauled her like a dog to death's corridor. The heavy chain clanked on the floor, biting into her neck and making it almost impossible to hold her head up. With every scrap of strength she could muster, she held it up to meet her fate head on, marching proudly past the rows of the worst deviants and *slogs* in the galaxy.

"What'd you do, sweet thing? Burn the muffins?" A particularly disgusting double-faced, four-legged Glitopuss taunted, coiling his long slimy tongue toward her. His genitals swelled and glistened grotesquely in the *weblinthium's* pulsing glow.

She veiled her eyes, looking away. Unfortunately, the view was no better wherever her glance fell.

"Maybe the Diva Goddess stuck that perky nose up in the air at the King," a single-breasted Pretadorn drawled. Sporting a single beady eye and three nostrils, she was as abominable as the Glitopuss.

"You take a wrong turn? The debutante ball is in the penthouse, at the top of the compound." Startled by the svelte, human voice, her gaze sought out the owner. He appeared to be the only man on the corridor. The inmate's amused gaze dissected each and every inch of her. He leaned against the *weblinthium* bars nonchalantly as if he was hanging out at the cantina. Mischief danced in the man's jade eyes, striking against his waist-length coal-black hair. He was simultaneously the most disreputable and sexiest male she'd ever seen, so much so, he made her forget to breathe. "Don't mind them. They never heard of manners."

And he had? Regardless of his handsome façade, she detected no evidence of his so-called manners. "You're on death's corridor because you have such sterling ones?" Siobhan returned the favor, letting her gaze drink him in. Tall enough to make her look up at him, the man had to stand at least six foot four inches. Broad shoulders tapered down to a narrow waist, slim hips, and powerful legs. Mocking intelligence smoldered in his disturbing gaze. Unkempt though he was, she grudgingly admitted the man was ruggedly handsome, with sculpted cheeks, a braided beard with faded beads strung through the two braids, and a high forehead, which his unruly locks insisted on tumbling over. He was one-hundred-eighty degrees opposite her fiancé's polished blonde figure. He wore the outfit of pirates, her sworn enemies.

"Just a little misunderstanding, sweet thing. My *attorneys* are working on my *appeal* as we speak."

Sweet thing? Hardly. If he'd heard the rumors of her supposed crime, he wouldn't waste a drop of charm on her. "Hope your attorneys are better than mine." Considering her own case, it was possible, if highly unlikely, he spoke the truth. Danger seeped from his every pore, mixed in with his scallywag charm. Charming men made her internal alarms whir out of control—they couldn't be trusted. Her father had tried to alliance her with several. Blatantly honest, she loved her straightforward Dennis. No artifice. No games. Thoroughly trustworthy, she could consign him her life. She had done so often and he had never let her down.

So where was he now?

Trying to find her, most definitely. She had been captured and arrested without due process...

The guard disabled the *weblinthium* force field in the cell across from the pirate, then unclasped the chain from her collar and shoved her inside. In a reverberating, mechanical voice, he said, "Better pray fast to your gods. Your execution will be at the rise of the third Balderian moon."

Why an electronic book?

We live in the Information Age—an exciting time in the history of human civilization in which technology rules supreme and continues to progress in leaps and bounds every minute of every hour of every day. For a multitude of reasons, more and more avid literary fans are opting to purchase e-books instead of paperbacks. The question to those not yet initiated to the world of electronic reading is simply: *why?*

1. *Price.* An electronic title at Ellora's Cave Publishing runs anywhere from 40-75% less than the cover price of the <u>exact same title</u> in paperback format. Why? Cold mathematics. It is less expensive to publish an e-book than it is to publish a paperback, so the savings are passed along to the consumer.

2. *Space.* Running out of room to house your paperback books? That is one worry you will never have with electronic novels. For a low one-time cost, you can purchase a handheld computer designed specifically for e-reading purposes. Many e-readers are larger than the average handheld, giving you plenty of screen room. Better yet, hundreds of titles can be stored within your new library—a single microchip. (Please note that Ellora's Cave does not endorse any specific brands. You can check our website at www.ellorascave.com

for customer recommendations we make available to new consumers.)

3. *Mobility.* Because your new library now consists of only a microchip, your entire cache of books can be taken with you wherever you go.

4. *Personal preferences are accounted for.* Are the words you are currently reading too small? Too large? Too...**ANNOYING**? Paperback books cannot be modified according to personal preferences, but e-books can.

5. *Innovation.* The way you read a book is not the only advancement the Information Age has gifted the literary community with. There is also the factor of what you can read. Ellora's Cave Publishing will be introducing a new line of interactive titles that are available in e-book format only.

6. *Instant gratification.* Is it the middle of the night and all the bookstores are closed? Are you tired of waiting days—sometimes weeks—for online and offline bookstores to ship the novels you bought? Ellora's Cave Publishing sells instantaneous downloads 24 hours a day, 7 days a week, 365 days a year. Our e-book delivery system is 100% automated, meaning your order is filled as soon as you pay for it.

Those are a few of the top reasons why electronic novels are displacing paperbacks for many an avid reader. As always, Ellora's Cave Publishing welcomes your questions and comments. We invite you to email us at service@ellorascave.com or write to us directly at: 1337 Commerce Drive, Suite 13, Stow OH 44224.

Discover for yourself why readers can't get enough of the multiple award-winning publisher Ellora's Cave. Whether you prefer e-books or paperbacks, be sure to visit EC on the web at www.ellorascave.com for an erotic reading experience that will leave you breathless.

WWW.ELLORASCAVE.COM

Printed in the United States
R1411400001B/R14114PG31178LVSX00001B/